Black McCarthy is despatched to INTERFOLD — The Time Travel Hotel to track down Eugenides.

His client, the Wolf, is on his back demanding progress as INTERFOLD keeps shifting time and place, throwing up residency and immigration anomalies as it does so.

Help of a kind is on hand via the Dwarf with the Horse, the Man Who Fell Through Floors, the Girl With Nine Lives, the Nurse With The Curse, and Joylin — the INTERFOLD receptionist.

But who is Eugenides? The Man Who Lived in a Vacuum Cleaner? The Man Who Dreamt He Was Dreaming? One of the other oddball residents? Is winding up naked in a sauna elevator in the Car Park at Infinity really going to help track him down?

Unfortunately for Black, his client is not the only one who wants Eugenides found, Black is possibly the worst detective money can buy and time is not only against him but ignoring all the usual rules.

"Not so much a whodunnit as a whydunnit or wheredunnit. Gleefully eccentric black humour and loop-the-loop sci-fi detective mayhem, with a cameo from TS Eliot, of course."
Sally Jenkinson

"If the prison governor forced you to read this book you probably have a decent chance with a human rights abuse claim."
Philip Brocklehurst

"The best Time Travel Detective Sex Comedy you'll ever read!"
Mark Steele-Mortimer

"Time Travel Hotel feels like a raft on a white-water river of of joyful anarchy. It's only as the plot starts to zip past that you find yourself turning your head and thinking, *Wait, did that just happen?*"
Anna Freeman

Typeset in dyslexie®
www.dyslexiefont.com

This edition published by Burning Eye Books 2015

www.burningeye.co.uk

@burningeyebooks

Burning Eye Books
15 West Hill, Portishead, BS20 6LG

ISBN 978 1 90913 652 6

Cover design by Dominic Brookman, kenoshadesign.com

CHAPTER ONE

1 Black McCarthy stood at the foot of the white marble steps leading to the main door to **INTERFOLD** — The Time Travel ~~Hotel~~ Republic, looking up at the towering chimneys illuminated against the clear night sky. He had awoken twelve hours earlier in a hotel in another city in another country to find the Wolf sitting watching him from the shadows. The Wolf had fixed him with shivering blue eyes and said:

"He is in Interfold."

"Interfold?"

"Yes, Interfold."

"The Time Travel Hotel?"

"Republic."

"What?"

"Republic."

"OK. The Time Travel ~~Hotel~~ Republic?"

"The same."

"Who is he?"

"All we have is a word. We assume it is his name."

"Assume?" Black had said.

"Yes."

"OK. What is the name?"

"Eugenides."

"How do I get there?" Black had begun to enquire, but the Wolf had already turned to fade into the shadows, leaving only an envelope on the floor as evidence of his existence. It contained a Cyprus Airways Apollo Class ticket from London to Larnaca, an old newspaper photograph which showed nothing that Black thought would be of use, and ten thousand dollars in cash.

He checked out of the hotel without incident. Took a taxi to Heathrow in good time. Checked in early and lingered in the lounge drinking complimentary coffee and reading complimentary newspapers until his flight was called. Flirted with a complimentary mahogany-haired and olive-skinned Cypriot stewardess throughout the five-hour flight but failed to extract a complimentary telephone number.

On arriving in Larnaca Black McCarthy walked down the steps of the aircraft into the balmy Mediterranean night, pausing only briefly to look up at the stars. He waited for his luggage in the baggage hall in bored silence, finding no reason to speak to any of his fellow passengers. Having retrieved his luggage, he made his way out of the airport in search of a taxi driver to take him to a place that he could not be sure would be there when they arrived.

He exited the terminal and paused, looking around. He hadn't visited Cyprus since... it seemed a lifetime ago. His memory reminded him that the taxi system at Larnaca airport was strictly regulated, but before he could follow his memory to the queue a man in a dark suit appeared beside him.

"I have been sent to collect you," he said.

McCarthy looked at the fellow standing beside him, who waited with hands held behind his back. A thin smile settled beneath a Syrian moustache. He was wearing a loosely knotted tie with thick black and red diagonal stripes. Black noticed a stain which may have been mayonnaise on the tie, noted the crumbs on his lapels.

"Sent to collect me?" Black asked.

"That is correct."

"You know where I am going?"

"Of course." The driver took the handle of Black's suitcase. "My car is over here." He turned away and gestured towards an ageing blue Mercedes. Black shrugged and followed him to the car.

"OK," he said. "How long will it take?"

"Less than one hour," the driver replied. He put Black's suitcase into the trunk of the Mercedes and opened a rear passenger door.

"I'll sit in the front," Black said, opening the door. The driver shrugged. Black got into the car.

It was an uneventful drive. Neither Black McCarthy nor his driver made any attempt at conversation. The driver because he had other things on his mind; Black because his thoughts were already leaping ahead to the task before him.

He was going to INTERFOLD — The Time Travel Hotel Republic in search of a man who might or might not be found under the name Eugenides. That was all Black knew. His task was simply to locate Eugenides and leave the consequences and repercussions to others, or so he told himself.

The driver took the road towards Nicosia for half an hour. The road quiet, the sound of the Mercedes joined only occasionally by other vehicles. Long before the outskirts of the city, the driver slowed and spun the car at a hard right angle to the main Nicosia road and turned onto a dusty track. They bumped along this would-be road without testing the suspension of the Mercedes. Outside the windows of the car, darkness was complete. The dust thrown up by the progress of the car obscured the way behind. Headlamp beams provided only feeble penetration of the road ahead.

This continued for some fifteen minutes before the driver manoeuvred the car to a sudden halt and killed the engine. Black was immediately tense and suspicious. His hand on the door release.

"We have arrived," his driver said impassively without looking at Black. Black offered no answer as he pulled the door release and stepped out into the night.

At first he could see nothing, but as the dust settled his eyes widened as he realised he had indeed arrived. The driver stepped out of the car and retrieved Black's suitcase, which he placed on the ground beside Black's feet. He stared at Black's shoes for a moment. He was wearing old Converse sneakers. The left one red, the right green.

"How much do I owe you?" Black asked.

The man ignored him and slipped back into the driver's seat of the Mercedes, gunned the engine and drove off into the night. Black watched him go and turned back to find himself at the foot of the white marble steps leading to the main door to INTERFOLD — The Time Travel ~~Hotel~~ Republic. He looked up at the ill-designed muddle of narrow, tapering, conical high-rise blocks growing out of and clustered around the body an old power station with four towering white chimneys illuminated against the clear night sky.

"Welcome to Interfold," he said.

2 The Man Who Lived in a Vacuum Cleaner woke late last Thursday, or it might have been yesterday, or not until three weeks next Tuesday. You see, this being INTERFOLD — The Time Travel ~~Hotel~~ Republic, it was difficult for him to be precise about something as imprecise as time. But even if he could not be exact about when this day was, or is, or soon will be, he was sure that something had changed, that something was new, that something was not exactly wrong but certainly... different.

For example, he was lying in bed. He hadn't done that for at least three of the five years that had passed since he had moved into 347B INTERFOLD APARTMENTS during INTERFOLD — The Time Travel ~~Hotel~~ Republic's brief stay in New York in the summer of 1922. He had not spent a single night in the bed for those three years because the bed was significantly smaller than he had become. It was also inconveniently positioned in a different room to his sofa and could only be reached via two dangerously narrow doorways. But not only was he lying in bed, he was also completely covered by what must have been a marquee-sized blanket, as his feet were not sticking out at one end and his head was covered at the other. "How very odd," he said to himself.

Cold with trepidation, he stretched out his arms in both directions and gasped. Neither hand had reached an edge of the bed. His mind reeled around, trying to comprehend; either he had been transported into a newly enlarged bed by a pack of weightlifting mice or... he had shrunk in the night.

Curious, he began to explore his body with his hands. He found a toned, muscular stomach, solid thighs that spoke of exercise, and a surprisingly large penis. *Perhaps this isn't all bad*, he thought. *Maybe I should take a look.*

He sat up, threw the blanket from the bed and leapt onto the floor. It was a long way down, but his solid thighs seemed up to the task and although the surprisingly large penis swung up to thud with some force against his stomach, the toned muscles against which it banged made this a pleasant, if fleeting, sensation.

He ran into the hallway, froze, and stared in alarm at the reflection in the mirror at the far end of the hall. The small male figure he saw looked facially related to the Man Who Lived in a Vacuum Cleaner, but this man was a slim miniature no more than three feet tall. Not only that, but as he stared he was sure the curious reflection was getting smaller. "What an odd mirror," he said to himself before the full realisation of his fate became clear.

He stared in disbelief.

He stared to outstare the obvious.

He stared as fear ran cold in his veins, shivered up every nerve, pounced on his composure and sent him wailing towards the mirror like a child.

He ran as hard as he could, but he knew that each step was getting smaller than the last. He kept running, but no matter how hard he ran the mirror reflected him getting smaller and smaller and smaller until he could see his reflection no more. He fell weeping to the floor no more than a few centimetres tall and still several metres from the mirror.

The Man Who Lived in a Vacuum Cleaner spent three weeks drifting naked, hungry and depressed around his giant's home, living on crumbs and condensation, before being rudely sucked into an industrial-grade vacuum cleaner. By good fortune he survived this violent process by the unreliable machine's choice of that very moment to expire. The **INTERFOLD** Cleaning Services operative, who was sanitising 347B **INTERFOLD APARTMENTS** so that it could be leased to a new tenant, kicked the vacuum cleaner in irritation.

"Damn heap o' junk," he mumbled.

By the end of that day the Man Who Lived in a Vacuum Cleaner's vacuum cleaner sat discarded in the service yard on the southern perimeter of **INTERFOLD** — The Time Travel ~~Hotel~~ Republic, complete with its new inhabitant.

The mysterious disappearance of the Man Who Lived in a

Vacuum Cleaner from 347B INTERFOLD APARTMENTS passed without the majority of the other inhabitants of INTERFOLD – The Time Travel ~~Hotel~~ Republic feeling compelled to register more than an eyebrow twitch of curiosity. The exception was the owner of TV Dinners Direct, who placed several press advertisements asking for information on his most valuable customer before filing for bankruptcy.

3 Doctor Klown was winding down after a long day in the INTERFOLD Emergency Room. He was trying to remember all the girls he'd like to get back, if only he could. But the thing that he always failed to grasp was that the river of time moved way too fast and the only girl he really wanted ruled out sexual congress on professional grounds.

"I am sorry, Doctor Klown," the Nurse with the Curse would say, "but it is out of the question for me to become involved with a colleague."

There was nothing left for him to do but sit by the bar or sing the blues at the regular Wednesday night Red Light Basement open-mic live blues band karaoke mega jam session. A carnival at which Doctor Klown came into his own, cutting a forlorn figure of desolation as he huffed and blew smooth blues from his trusted harmonica into the Red Light Basement's trademark retro microphone.

"And I feel like I'm stuck on a rock," he sang, "at the edge of a waterfall, wondering how far down I need to fall before I drown." Before blowing his silver harmonica again like his soul was simmering in the embers. Beautiful.

As he sang he frowned to see what looked like a large black horse and a small man enter the bar and order drinks. "Oh, well," he said to himself, "nothing all that unusual around here."

4 The Dwarf with the Horse was migrating north when, overcome with thirst, he settled down to lounge beside the bar of the Red Light Basement, a seedy drinking establishment located in the basement of the north-west corner of INTERFOLD – The Time Travel ~~Hotel~~ Republic.

"That's about as far," he said to the barman, "as I am going to go for now." He turned and looked around the bar, nodding approvingly at Doctor Klown's blues.

"Going underground, going underground," Pedro, a fine black stallion, sang beside him, tapping a hoof.

"Stop that, Pedro," the Dwarf ordered. "What do you want to drink?"

"Pint," said the Horse.

"A pint for me and a half for the Horse," the Dwarf told the barman.

"It's all right here," Pedro said, nodding, as the barman poured their drinks and placed them on the bar.

"Good work, Moe," the Dwarf said, handing over some cash.

"My name's Dave," the barman replied, handing him some change.

"More beers when you're ready, Moe," Black McCarthy called from further along the bar.

"My name's Dave," Moe repeated.

"Just serve the beers, Moe," Pedro said, eyeing his half with anticipation.

"But my name is Dave," Dave said again just in case anyone was listening, which they weren't.

"Whatever, Moe." Pedro formed a straw with his long pink tongue, dipped it in his beer and emptied the glass with a single loud SLURP. Moe and Black McCarthy turned to the Dwarf in disgust.

He shrugged. "Sorry about that. Damn horse has the manners of a farm animal."

"Just line them up, shorty," Pedro said, grinning to show his formidable set of teeth. "I've got my drinking legs on this evening."

The Dwarf nodded at Moe to repeat the order. Moe had just begun pouring Pedro another half when the Man Who Fell Through Floors crashed through the ceiling and landed astride Pedro with a thump.

"What the..." Pedro started and bucked the dazed guy off his back. The Man Who Fell Through Floors found himself dumped on the floor, wide-eyed and a little less freaked out than the last time it had happened, but pretty freaked out all the same. He rose shakily to his feet and staggered to the bar and climbed onto a stool beside Black McCarthy.

"It doesn't matter how many times that happens," he said to Black, "I am never going to get used to it."

"Get the man a beer, Moe," Black McCarthy said; he

was in a generous mood despite making little progress in the first week of his search for Eugenides. Moe sighed in defeat, placed Pedro's pint on the bar in front of him and began pouring a further pint for the Man Who Fell Through Floors.

"Cheers, Moe," Pedro said, and forming his long pink tongue into a straw he once more emptied the glass in one loud SLURP.

"My name is Dave," said Dave.

"Whatever, Moe," the Horse slurred, blinking slowly, before crashing sideways to the floor unconscious.

"Damn horse never could hold his drink," the Dwarf said without turning to look at Pedro. "Who's the babe, Moe?" he asked, nodding at a dark-haired woman in a red dress. Dave ignored him and walked away to serve another customer.

5   Alex from Mars, hanging around the bar in a tight red dress and a push-up bra, remembered all the guys who never came back; if only one would. The thing that she had failed to grasp was that, INTERFOLD time being what it was, the only man she had ever really wanted was buried on another planet. There was nothing left for her to do but to put away another vodka or two and accept the invitation of a revived Pedro and the Dwarf to some:

"Unlimited three-way action, baby!" Pedro winked, twitching his tail seductively. "Goddamn it, Moe, get this lovely lady another drink!"

"I've told you already, buddy," Moe said, "my name is Dave."

"Whatever, Moe, whatever," Alex muttered, watching the Doc, shades in place, harp in hand as he crooned and crooned and crooned. "Who's the singer?"

"He's a doctor from the ER upstairs," Dave replied.

"He's pretty good," Alex said, impressed.

"Yeah, not bad. Comes in every Wednesday night for the open mic."

"Can anyone sing?"

"Sure can, but I'd give it a miss unless you are good. This crowd won't stand for second-rate."

"And who are the band?"

"Walter. Used to be known as Walter and His Softy

Chums, but they shortened it a year ago. Came on board in London in the spring of '86."

"London?"

"London. You know — capital of England?"

"Oh, yeah — sure." She turned her gaze back to the Doc, decided she had said too much already.

6 A few minutes earlier, or maybe later that week sometime or — hell, I don't know — sometime in 1993, outside in the service yard on the southern perimeter of **INTERFOLD** — The Time Travel ~~Hotel~~ Republic, the Bag Lady Who Was Thrown Away was scavenging in the garbage as usual when she discovered the Man Who Lived in a Vacuum Cleaner's vacuum cleaner home and claimed it as her own. Foraging through the dust bag for anything she could sell, she found only him.

She stared at the little man with a surprisingly large penis who stood in the centre of her palm looking up at her. He waved his arms in a friendly sort of way to indicate he was human. Smiling back at him in wonder, she pinched the surprisingly large penis between forefinger and thumb and lifted the little man up above her head. Opening her mouth wide — she dropped him in and tried to swallow him whole.

She gagged immediately and choked. The little man jammed in her throat, fighting for his life.

The Bag Lady Who Was Thrown Away staggered down some steps that happened to be in front of her. Her face growing red, her hands clutched to her burning throat. A fire door stood ajar. She slammed it aside and stumbled through. She was in a corridor. Up ahead a couple were snogging beside a stack of yellow crates holding empty beer bottles, the man's hand high under the short skirt of the one-legged girl. The Bag Lady shoved past them and crashed through another fire door into the Red Light Basement.

7 Doctor Klown stopped singing as a filthy woman wearing black plastic trash bags staggered towards him, clutching her throat. He leapt from the stage, spun her around and expertly applied the Heimlich manoeuvre to clear her airway. He held his breath to keep the stench of his patient at bay as, to demonstrate her gratitude, the Bag Lady turned round and head-butted the doctor squarely on the nose.

"Bloody hell!" Doctor Klown spluttered, holding his nose as blood splurged down his face.

"Bastard!" the Bag Lady shrieked, grabbing him by the throat and throwing her weight at him, knocking him to the floor. "Rapist! Molester!"

"Hey, buddy," Black McCarthy said to the Man Who Fell Through Floors, "could you give me a hand?" He strode towards the struggling Doc and Bag Lady.

"Come on, lady," he said, "give the guy a break. He was trying to do you a favour." With the assistance of the Man Who Fell Through Floors he dragged a writhing and screaming Bag Lady back out through the fire exit and dumped her roughly into a large pile of garbage bags.

"Wow," the Man Who Fell Through Floors said, holding his nose, "she really stinks." He looked at the Bag Lady, who was blending in with her bed of garbage, not moving. "Do you think she's OK?"

Black McCarthy looked at the reclining Bag Lady and shrugged.

"Probably just drunk," he said. "Let her sleep it off. She looks like she's used to it."

He turned to walk away before he realised he had not introduced himself to the Man Who Fell Through Floors. He offered his right hand.

"By the way, my name is Black McCarthy."

8 Distracted by the antics of the Bag Lady, no one had noticed that the Man Who Lived in a Vacuum Cleaner had been expelled from her throat. He flew through the air and landed with a plop in Alex's vodka. Luckily she took it with ice, lemon and a little tonic, which helped keep him afloat until a rescue could be launched.

Turning back to her drink, Alex from Mars was surprised to find an unconscious little man with a surprisingly large penis floating in her vodka. She dipped her fingers into the glass and pulled him out.

"Story of my life," she said to herself; "finally find a man with a penis as long as his arm and it is still too small to be worth attention." Since arriving on Earth she had been disappointed by the apparent incompatibility of the minuscule members sported by most Earthlings and her roomy Martian vagina. She held the Man Who Lived in a Vacuum Cleaner up to her ear to check if he was breathing and found he was snoring soundly. Probably drunk, she thought.

"What you got there, honey?" the Dwarf with the Horse asked, stretching to see what was in her hand.

"Oh, nothing." She smiled and slipped the Man Who Lived in a Vacuum Cleaner into her handbag.

9 The Man Who Lived in a Vacuum Cleaner woke with a furious headache but otherwise unharmed. Hunting around Alex's handbag he found some aspirin. Unsure of the dose for a man of his stature, he took a tentative lick of a pill. It was revolting. There was also a half-eaten bar of chocolate on hand; he broke off a crumb and ate the best meal he had eaten in a month.

Having pulled himself up to the open zip of Alex's bag, he stuck his head out as he munched. He pushed aside a fragrant red Lycra garment to clear his view and was stunned by what he saw.

Before him was a large and, he suspected, expensive hotel bedroom. A hotel bedroom in which a dark-haired and rather beautiful, he thought, woman with an apparently cavernous vagina and the longest nipples he had ever seen was kneeling on the end of the bed with her buttocks spread wide. She was being rigorously penetrated by a fine black stallion whilst simultaneously fellating a swarthy midget who was lying on the bed with his hands behind his head wearing nothing more than a pointed black goatee, some cheap sunglasses and a large smile.

"Things," the Man Who Lived in a Vacuum Cleaner said to himself, taking another bite of chocolate to ease his hangover, "appear to be looking up."

CHAPTER TWO

The Man Who Dreamt He Was Dreaming was dreaming he was dreaming. He had fallen into a drunken sleep after his business had become bankrupt and girlfriend had left him for the seventh time for being a misogynistic pig. He hadn't disagreed with her diagnosis. He did indeed treat her badly, and always had. Yes, he was an inconsiderate and brutal lover. He did take her for granted, and essentially she was correct when she accused him of considering her a simple source of convenient sex.

"But," he asked her, "if all that is such a problem, why do you keep coming back?"

Her only response was to leave. In doing so she chose the unconventional method of throwing herself out of the window of his apartment on the thirteenth floor of INTERFOLD. He ran to the window as she disappeared.

"Why can't you use the fucking elevator like any normal person?" he yelled after her, before walking into the kitchen to pour a cold beer.

"She only does it to piss you off," he told himself. "It is not as if she is even in danger of succeeding."

This was true. He knew it, she knew it and Doctor Klown, who usually tended to the superficial wounds she sustained in indulging in what would to any normal person be fatal behaviour, knew it as well.

He did what he considered the right thing under the circumstances and drank himself if not into unconsciousness then certainly into a very deep sleep. This had more to do with the collapse of his business TV Dinners Direct than with the by-now-commonplace behaviour of his girlfriend. The business had been at the edge of insolvency for months and would have crashed earlier if it had not been for the fantastic appetite of his most valuable and valued customer. The sudden disappearance of the Man Who Lived in a Vacuum Cleaner had been the fatal blow and the business had sunk beneath the burden of its debts within weeks.

The Man Who Dreamt He Was Dreaming had taken the failure of his business badly and took to drinking heavily, sleeping deeply and treating his girlfriend with an even greater degree of calculated indifference than was usual. He didn't blame her. He blamed the continual spontaneous relocation of INTERFOLD – The Time Travel Hotel Republic around the world. This had resulted in an ever-changing array of restaurants being permanently on hand, offering a fantastic array of global cuisine around the clock. Due to the limited geography of INTERFOLD – The Time Travel Hotel Republic, most were quite happy to offer a delivery service while INTERFOLD was in town. As a result the Man Who Dreamt He Was Dreaming's once novel and exclusive business had struggled to survive. Even once the lurches backwards and forwards in time had become erratic, the average INTERFOLD resident had felt no need to fall back on the stable presence of his homespun meal delivery service.

As one of the founding residents of INTERFOLD – The Time Travel Hotel Republic, he took this personally. Unlike the transient residents who had made INTERFOLD their home, he had been in on the adventure from the beginning. He had been amongst the crowd that had stormed the redundant power station in a protest that had started out as a political statement against the government of the day and had ended with a declaration of independence.

In his opinion **INTERFOLD** was not the revolutionary paradise it had once been. Since they had started letting every damn Johnny Foreigner who felt like moving in take up residence, the place had lost its edge. If it were up to him he would kick the whole lot of them out and start again. Send them back where they came from — and that included the dozy tart who had thrown herself out of his window in a sad attempt to make a point. Although what point he really couldn't be bothered to work out.

In the dream he was dreaming it was raining. He was in a car driving through the streets of the town where he had lived in the years before **INTERFOLD** was created. It was dark, the view of the dream obscured by rain and the intermittent orange glow of street lamps. He turned into the narrow avenue of Victorian terraced houses where he had lived and stopped outside the house that had been his home. Immediately he was inside and ascending the stairs. No lights were on. Feeling the way in the dark, he turned the handle of the door into his bedroom. The door swung wide open in agonising slow motion. Inside he saw himself lying in bed with a very pale dark-haired girl kneeling on top of him wearing only a black bra and panties. Her face obscured by her wet hair. As he watched she pulled a large silver knife from behind her and began stabbing him manically in the chest over and over and over again.

He woke with a jolt. It was dark. Grey light hung heavy in the room. The same room he had entered in the dream. There was an odd electric stillness around him.

"I'm still dreaming," he said aloud, recognising the unreality of the scene.

He dreamt himself settling back down into the bed. He dreamt himself closing his eyes. He dreamt himself dropping back down through layer upon layer of black sleep into a deeper layer of dreaming.

CHAPTER THREE

1 "Doctor Klown, what have you been doing?" the Nurse
with the Curse asked in alarm as Doctor Klown, a blood-
soaked handkerchief held over his battered nose, walked into
the ER accompanied by Black McCarthy and the Man Who
Fell Through Floors.

"He was head-butted by a bag lady," Black McCarthy
said. "I'm Black McCarthy, by the way."

He offered his hand in introduction. The Nurse with the
Curse turned to look at Black, took his hand and shook it
gently, holding his gaze for what seemed to both of them to
be no more than a moment but was in fact long enough for
the Man Who Fell Through Floors to find it necessary to
clear his throat loudly.

"Sit down and let me look at your nose," the Nurse with
the Curse said to Doctor Klown, although she continued to
look at Black McCarthy.

Doctor Klown sat down and reluctantly removed his hand from his nose to allow the Nurse with the Curse to examine it.

"There is no break, Doctor," she said, "but you will be badly bruised. I will clean you up a little." She began to gently wipe the blood from his face with a swab. "Why did this lady do such a thing?"

"He made the mistake of saving her life," Black McCarthy said, smiling.

"Saving her life?" the Nurse with the Curse said, confused.

"She stumbled into the Red Light Basement choking and the Doc helped her out — only she wasn't overly grateful and headbutted him in thanks," the Man Who Fell Through Floors added.

"That dreadful place," the Nurse with the Curse said. "I do not understand why you need to spend so much time in there." She cast a disappointed and disapproving look at Black McCarthy.

"Good blues and good beer are difficult things for a man to resist," he suggested. The Man Who Fell Through Floors nodded in agreement.

The Nurse with the Curse shook her head, frowning, and continued cleaning the blood from Doctor Klown's face.

"You guys head back," Doctor Klown told the other two. "I am on duty in half an hour anyway. Thanks for your help, though; I appreciate it." He didn't like the apparent attraction between Black and the Nurse with the Curse. The sooner Black left, the better.

"OK. If you're sure," the Man Who Fell Through Floors said.

"Yeah. Don't worry; you guys get on," the doctor assured him.

"All right, buddy," Black McCarthy said, "but I think I'll come back tomorrow and ask your colleague here a few questions — if that's OK with you?" he added, looking at the Nurse with the Curse.

"Questions?" she asked. "What about?"

"I am looking for a man named Eugenides. I need to verify that he is still located in Interfold. I'd like to talk it over, see if you can help in any way."

"In any way?"

"In any way at all."

"I cannot break patient confidentiality," she told him.

"Don't worry. I know all I need to know about him apart from whether he has been seen in Interfold inside the last month."

"I am on duty at two pm," the Nurse with the Curse said.

"Why don't I come in around one and buy you lunch?" Black offered. "We can talk and you can see whether you can assist."

"Without breaking patient confidentiality."

"Without breaking patient confidentiality," he assured her.

"All right," she said, holding his gaze once more, "one it is."

"I'll look forward to it," Black said. "It was good to meet you. You take it easy now, Doc."

"Yeah, I'm fine. See you guys." Doctor Klown waved a hand as the Man Who Fell Through Floors and Black McCarthy walked back towards the elevator.

2   The Man Who Fell Through Floors and Black McCarthy stood waiting for the elevator to take them back down to the Red Light Basement. Black couldn't stop smiling.

"She's really something," he said.

"She's certainly beautiful," the Man Who Fell Through Floors agreed, "but there is a terrible sadness in her."

"Sadness?" Black asked.

"She has had a tragic life," the Man Who Fell Through Floors said. "Have you not heard her story?"

"No," said Black, "I've only been here a week. I didn't even know she existed until today. What's the story?"

"Her Interfold name is 'the Nurse with the Curse'."

"What kind of curse?" Black asked.

"Sin 322."

"Sin 322?"

"Sin 322," the Man Who Fell Through Floors said again as they stepped into the elevator. Black McCarthy did not understand but let him continue. "She's a Tuareg princess."

"That explains..." Black began.

"The dark skin and eyes as deep as the desert?"

"Exactly."

"And that way she has of looking at you like she is studying the contours of your soul."

"Has she been in Interfold for long?" Black asked.

"Longer than I have. The story goes that her father was a powerful tribal leader. He had arranged for her to be married to the son of an ally. The wedding was a magnificent affair, but the next morning she was found distraught with her husband dead beside her. No cause of death was apparent and her magnificent wedding was followed swiftly by a funeral. She was only sixteen at the time."

"So what had happened?" Black asked.

"Sin 322."

"Sin 322?"

"Sin 322."

Black still didn't understand, but he wasn't the kind of man who liked to draw attention to such things. "So what happened next?"

"Her father, keen to draw a line under the first wedding, arranged for her to be married to the younger brother of her husband exactly one year after the first wedding. Once more there was a magnificent wedding accompanied by a feast so extravagant that people would talk of it for months to come."

"But I get the feeling husband number two is no longer with her?"

"Afraid not. The same thing happened. The next morning her second husband was found dead beside her without injury or cause. He was in every way a healthy young dead man."

"Wow, that's some curse," Black said.

"Sin 322?"

"Sin 322."

"It's the worst there is," the Man Who Fell Through Floors said.

"So how did she come to be in Interfold?" Black asked.

"Well, her father didn't give up. She was still a beautiful seventeen-year-old and he was a powerful man with alliances to forge. So he kept trying to arrange marriages for her."

"Did he succeed?"

"Another five times."

"And what happened?"

"Exactly the same thing. Seven times she was married and on seven mornings after her wedding nights her husband lay dead."

"With no identifiable cause of death?"

"Every one a healthy young dead man." The Man Who Fell Through Floors shook his head sadly.

"That Sin 322, eh?" Black said, hoping The Man Who Fell Through Floors would elaborate.

"I know. It's a killer," the Man Who Fell Through Floors said and fell through the floor of the elevator, leaving nothing but a small puff of cartoon dust behind him. Black McCarthy watched the dust gently disperse and continued to descend, alone.

3 Back in the ER the Nurse with the Curse was plugging Doctor Klown's nose with cotton wool. It was driving him nuts. The way she leant over him with her deep dark bosom an inviting chasm. How he longed to throw himself to its mercy. But she was cool and indifferent as usual.

"There you are, Doctor. That should stop the bleeding." She stood back with hands on hips. "But you really should try to give up fighting with strange ladies, for a week or two at least."

"Very funny," the doctor muttered, scowling. The Nurse with the Curse stifled a giggle. "Any patients?"

"Just one so far."

"Anyone we know?" Doctor Klown asked. The INTERFOLD ER had a number of regular customers. He stood up and followed the Nurse towards the curtained areas where patients were examined.

"Oh, yes," the Nurse said. "The Girl with Nine Lives."

"Again?" asked Doctor Klown.

"Again," confirmed the Nurse with the Curse.

"How did she do it this time?"

"I don't know for sure. She is still unconscious, but it looks like she jumped out of a window again."

"You think she'd try and be a little more inventive, if only for our sake. I guess we'd better take a good look at her." Doctor Klown raised his eyebrows and pulled back a curtain. There was no one behind it.

"Doctor," the Nurse with the Curse said. Doctor Klown turned towards her. "The patient is in here." She pulled back the curtain of the next examination area to reveal the Girl with Nine Lives lying unconscious on the bed.

It had only been a few months since the last time she had thrown herself out of a window high on the side of what had once been an iconic power station on the south bank of the Thames, and she therefore looked only a little different. A little thinner, maybe, a little more worn down. She lay unmoving as Doctor Klown looked at her, shaking his head.

"Why does she put herself through this time after time?"

"I think she is addicted to the drama," the Nurse with the Curse said, "or perhaps the rush of adrenalin as she falls, or maybe she simply does it because she can."

"And how many times is this now?" Doctor Klown asked, still looking at his patient. The Girl with Nine Lives lay motionless, her face an alabaster mask, her clothes wet and red.

"I don't know, Doctor," the Nurse with the Curse said. "Many times."

"I think, Nurse, that she is fortunate in two ways."

"How so, Doctor?"

"One, that we are not counting, and two..."

"That she is not a cat?"

"Indeed yes, Nurse, indeed yes," he said, "but she certainly knows how to bleed, so I think we had better cut away these wet clothes and check that tonight is not the night she has succeeded in really injuring herself."

4 A week earlier or early one bitter morning in January 1973, Black McCarthy had walked up the white marble steps that led to the main entrance to INTERFOLD — The Time Travel Hotel Republic and continued through the door. He strolled into the foyer of the INTERFOLD Hotel, which was conveniently located in the main entrance hall of the former power station, and approached the reception desk.

"Joylin," he said, noting the name badge of the Vietnamese girl behind the counter, "I believe you are expecting me."

"Possibly, sir," she said, looking at the man who stood before her wearing a creased pin-striped suit jacket paired with scruffy jeans and a Sonic Youth "Goo" T-shirt. She looked at his cropped hair, the single gold earring in his left ear, three days of stubble and the mismatched Converse sneakers. "Your name?"

"Black McCarthy."

"Let me see..." She tapped at the keyboard. Looked at the reservations screen. "No..." She paused. "Nothing in the name of McCarthy."

"It's spelt with two C's," he offered.

"I am sorry, sir, but I have nothing under that name with any number of C's. What is the purpose of your visit?" She smiled and looked up at Black's face with her large hazel eyes.

"I am looking for... someone," Black said.

"Ah. You are the Detective Who Has Never Solved a Case."

"Technically that is correct, but it is a very complicated business."

"If you say so."

"Solving is not the entire game," Black explained. "I just find people. If there is solving to be done I leave that to others."

"Of course." She smiled broadly to herself and flicked a brief glance back at Black. "You will be in Suite 9762. I think you will find it to your satisfaction. All of our rooms are world-class."

"I don't doubt," Black said. "I understand the service is also..." — he paused, meeting her eyes — "unbeatable." He snapped his Black Amex down on the counter and threw her his most charming smile.

"Thank you, sir," she said, holding his eyes as she pushed the card back towards him, "but your account is taken care of." She placed a similar black card next to the Amex. "This will allow you to access your room and other permitted areas of INTERFOLD."

"What interests me more," he said, leaning forward with a raised eyebrow, "are the areas to which permission is withheld."

"To some areas, sir," Joylin replied, "permission must be earned before access is granted."

"What I meant, Joylin," Black continued, speaking slow and low, "is — um — is it possible for you to have yourself sent up to my room with my suitcase?" He left his right eyebrow raised in emphasis.

"Mr McCarthy," Joylin replied in a quiet yet firm voice, "that is something to which even a Black Amex will not grant you access." She smiled as if entertained rather than offended.

"Come, come, Joylin," Black said. "If I know one thing, it is that everyone has a vice, and" — he paused — "a price."

"Mr McCarthy," Joylin repeated, "I do not deny that I

may well have both, but why not start by offering to buy me a drink?"

An hour later Black McCarthy sat at the bar in the Red Light Basement. Joylin was at his side.

"Hey, Moe," she called to Dave the barman, "a shot of tequila for me and a beer for Mr McCarthy."

"You can call me Black," Black said over his shoulder as he watched the stage. A thin blonde was dancing a languid striptease to a heavy blues riff laid down by a bored-looking Walter. She turned her back on the crowded bar and removed her bra. Bent over forwards and peeled off her panties. Tossed them over her shoulder into the waiting hands of a drinker. Turned back to face her audience and as a finale removed the lower half of her left leg, tossed this in the direction of her underwear and fell swiftly onto her back with her uneven limbs spread apart. The band crunched to a halt. Black turned back to face Joylin as she downed her tequila. She placed the glass on the bar in front of her with a deliberate thud.

"Her," she said, nodding in the direction of the stage, "I can have sent up to your room like a piece of luggage." She stood up, tipped Black's beer into his lap and left.

A week later Black McCarthy walked back into the Red Light Basement and sat on the same bar stool as the same girl undressed on stage.

"Hey, Moe," he called to Dave, "has Floors not come back in yet?"

"Not yet," Moe replied. "I thought he was with you."

"Yeah, he was," Black said. "He fell through the floor of the elevator on the way back down from the ER."

"No way," Moe said, incredulous. "Not twice in one night. That must really piss him off."

"You bet," Black said. "Maybe I should go and look for him."

"No point," Dave advised. "He could be anywhere. Let me get you a beer."

"Yeah, sure, thanks," Black said over his shoulder, his mind already elsewhere. It hadn't been a good week. He was no closer to locating Eugenides than he had been the moment he had arrived in INTERFOLD. Getting on the wrong side of Joylin, a potentially useful source of information, had not been a good move. The Man Who Fell Through Floors looked like a useful contact, but he had gone astray before Black had had a chance to question him. He watched the stage and began to wonder whether he should have the one-legged girl sent up to his room again.

5 In the ER Doctor Klown had left the Nurse with the Curse to attend to removing the wet and bloody clothes from the Girl with Nine Lives. Piece by piece and layer by layer the Nurse cut and peeled until the Girl lay wearing only a sheen of blood. With a sigh the Nurse began slowly and carefully to clean the blood from her skin, searching for signs of serious injury. She found none and by the time Doctor Klown returned the Girl with Nine Lives lay clean and naked.

"She is ready for you to examine her now, Doctor," the Nurse with the Curse said.

"Thank you, Nurse," Doctor Klown replied, looking at the Girl. "Any change in her status?"

"No, no change and no obvious reason for the amount of blood."

"How very odd," Doctor Klown said, "and yet how very normal for our patient. Help me turn her, please, Nurse." Between them they turned the girl onto her side. The doctor gave her back a cursory examination. "Nothing here. Not even bruising. Quite incredible."

"Can I get some help here?" A male voice called from outside in the corridor.

"Can you see who that is, please, Nurse?" the Doc instructed the Nurse as he began to carefully examine the head of the Girl with Nine Lives. The Nurse stepped out through the curtain.

Doctor Klown stood back, satisfied that his patient was unconscious but otherwise unharmed. "How unusual," he commented to himself, noticing for the first time the odd pubic hair of the Girl with Nine Lives, which formed a thick, luxurious delta and was striped like a badger.

Without thinking he stretched out a hand and gently stroked its texture with a single fingertip. It felt soft and expensive. How fascinating, he thought as another finger joined the first and he stroked deeper into the striped layers of thick hair.

"DOCTOR KLOWN!" the Nurse with the Curse exclaimed as she saw where he had his hand. "What are you doing?"

"Ah, Nurse. Good." He cleared his throat as his face

reddened with embarrassment. "Just, er... is there" — he paused — "another patient?"

The Nurse with the Curse moved to cover the naked Girl with Nine Lives with a sheet before saying, "Yes, Doctor, she has just been brought in. Follow me."

Behind a curtain across the corridor from the Girl with Nine Lives lay the Bag Lady Who Was Thrown Away. Doctor Klown was appalled.

"Not her again!" he said in disgust.

"Is this the one who hit your nose?" The Nurse with the Curse stifled a laugh. "She doesn't seem very dangerous."

"No," the Doc said, looking at his patient, "more pathetic really, and, from the smell of her, quite drunk. Why don't you clean her up, Nurse, and find her somewhere to sleep? If you feel there is reason for me to see her again, let me know. In the meantime I am going to get some coffee." He turned and slipped between the curtains, leaving the Nurse with the Curse shaking her head.

He went into his office and closed the door. Leant his back against it and closed his eyes. In his mind he pictured the striped delta-pelt of the Girl with Nine Lives. Imagined his fingers probing deep between her silken threads. He raised the culpable fingers to his lips.

"Coffee," he said aloud to break his train of thought. He poured himself a dark cup and took a deep slug to erase the taste of his fingers from his mind. He shook his head slowly. "What a night."

6 "He went into a bookstore, leaving his wife outside," Dave the barman was telling Black McCarthy.

"A bookstore?"

"Yeah, a bookstore. In Bath."

"In Bath? Which one? I know Bath quite well."

"I have no idea." Moe put a fresh bottle of beer in front of McCarthy.

"Thanks. Carry on," Black said.

"As I was saying," Dave continued, "the Man Who Fell Through Floors went into a bookstore, leaving his wife outside. There's a particular novel by Kundera that he was looking for, having lent his copy to a sometime friend who never returned it."

"Which one?" Black asked.

"Which friend?"

"No. Which Kundera novel?"

"I'm not sure that he mentioned it," Moe said.

"Probably *The Unbearable Lightness of Being*," Black offered.

"No, it was *The Book of Laughter and Forgetting*," Dave said.

"I thought you said he didn't mention it," Black said.

Moe shrugged. "I just remembered. So he's looking through the shelves, tracking along, you know, looking for K, Kafka, Kellerman, Kundera, whatever, but they've moved the store around and he can't find it."

"Happens all the time."

"Of course it does. So he asks a girl who looks like she works there where he can find Kundera's *Book of Laughter and Forgetting*. She says he needs to look in the basement and points to a doorway through which a staircase descends to the basement. He follows her advice and down he goes."

"Did he find it?" Black said.

"No, he did not," Dave replied. "He follows the staircase round a couple of turns, walks without question through the door at the bottom of the stairs and is surprised to find himself in what appears to be someone's sitting room."

"So what happened?"

"He's standing there, a little taken aback, when this young guy walks into the room from another direction. The guy stares at Floors in total surprise. 'Who the hell are you?' he says to Floors. Floors says, 'I am very sorry; the assistant upstairs sent me down here. I am looking for *The Book of Laughter and Forgetting*.' 'What assistant?' the guy asks, clearly confused. 'In the bookstore upstairs,' Floors explains. 'But there is no bookstore upstairs,' the guy comes back. Floors is confused, says, 'You must be mistaken; I have just walked down these stairs from the bookstore upstairs.' He turns to gesture to the stairs he walked down only moments before." Moe paused for effect. "But they have gone."

"Gone?" Black asked.

"Gone. No stairs, no doorway, no bookstore."

"What did he do?"

"He turns back to the young guy. I'm guessing he goes a pale shade of grey. But there is an alarm bell ringing in his head somewhere. He stares at the young guy and he can't explain why but he says to him, 'What's the date?' The young guy answers with a date that is ten years before the date that Floors started the day in. Floors gets a little more pale. 'But that is ten years ago,' he says. The young guy starts to back away towards the telephone. He thinks he has a madman in his house. And just at the very moment when the guy's hand touches the phone, that's when it happens."

"What happens?" asked Black, taking a slug from his beer.

"He falls through the floor for the first time. Bam. Down he goes, falling and falling. Comes right through the ceiling over there." He pointed to the stage. "Knocks a one-legged dancer out cold."

"How long ago was this?" Black asked.

"Three years, give or take a month or so."

"And he's stayed in Interfold ever since?" Black asked.

"Of course. What else can he do? He fell back into the past and then landed here, closer to his future but not close enough. His current self is still out there living the life he has already lived. Until enough time passes or we get a relocation that works for him, he's stuck. If he's lucky Interfold will relocate into his close future and he can step back into his life and carry on."

"What a nightmare." Black shook his head and took another slug of beer.

"You bet. Even if he can get back, how does he explain to his wife that he spent several years in Interfold while she was waiting for him outside a bookstore in Bath one afternoon?" As he spoke the room trembled and a deep bass rumble echoed throughout INTERFOLD.

"What was that?" Black asked, slipping off the bar stool and standing up, taking a couple of steps back and looking up at the ceiling.

"Here we go," Moe said. "Relocation time."

"Already?" Black asked. "I've only been here a week; I thought I'd get longer."

The room trembled again and the deep bass rumble repeated and then faded. Silence settled.

"Is that it?" Black asked.

"That's it," Dave said, looking past him. "Never takes long."

"And it's completely random?"

"Completely. No idea where we'll be next or when." He paused, looking over Black's shoulder. "Your man's back," he said, nodding at the approaching figure of the Man Who Fell Through Floors. He was covered in dust.

"What happened to you?" Black asked him.

"Got stuck at the bottom of the elevator shaft," he said. "Give me a beer, Moe. My throat is full of spiders."

"My name is..." Moe began to say, but he thought better of it when he caught the blazing eyes of the Man Who Fell Through Floors. "One beer coming up."

"Have we relocated?" the Man Who Fell Through Floors asked.

"Seems that way," Black replied.

"Any idea where we are yet, or when?"

Black shrugged, shaking his head.

"Hey, Moe," the Man Who Fell Through Floors called to Dave, who had moved away to serve another customer, "any idea where we are yet?"

"Not yet. Why don't you take a look? I'll see if I can get a time reference," Moe said.

"Come on," the Man Who Fell Through Floors said to Black. He walked across the bar and through the same fire exit through which the Bag Lady Who Was Thrown Away had entered earlier that evening. At the end of a short corridor they passed through a fire door and ascended a few steps.

Beyond the perimeter fence, which marked the boundary of the service area behind INTERFOLD, they could see a large winding river, and beyond that a town illuminated and quiet under a clear sky.

"1968," Moe said, appearing beside them, sniffing the air. "Any idea where we are?" It smelled of chocolate.

"It looks," the Man Who Fell Through Floors said, appalled, "like Keynsham."

"Keynsham?" Black McCarthy said.

"Keynsham?" Moe echoed.

"Keynsham," the Man Who Fell Through Floors said. "Of course we are in bloody Keynsham." He turned and slammed the fire door aside and disappeared back into the Red Light Basement.

"What's so bad about Keynsham?" Black asked Dave.

"No idea," Moe said. "No idea at all."

CHAPTER FOUR

The Man Who Dreamt He Was Dreaming was dreaming he was dreaming. He had been asleep for more than a week, and although he knew that he was dreaming he was dreaming, in the suspended chronology of sleep he had no idea that, outside his mind, days were slipping past.

He had descended into a deep and complex dream layer where he was reliving the pre-**INTERFOLD** years of his life. He had often idly wondered how his life would have been different if he had taken up opportunities he had allowed to pass. Decisions he might reverse, and girls he might have... especially girls he might have... and now he was playing out events from his life to see what might have been.

The girl in the wet pink panties, for instance. He had always wondered why he had let that moment pass. When the sea had risen high on her thighs she had pulled up her skirt to reveal a pink triangle wetted dark by the sea.

"I'm getting a bit wet," she had said, looking down.

But the guys had been calling him from the boat, and he had turned, distracted, and when he had looked back she had been walking back to the beach and for some reason, some unfathomable reason, he had followed the guys out to the boat rather than the girl in the wet pink panties back to the beach.

But not this time; this time it would be different, for although he was dreaming he was dreaming, he had a degree of control. He couldn't stop dreaming, he had found, but he could dream himself up and down between dreams and he could steer the dream into a situation from his past.

And so he steered the dream back to that day at the beach when the girl in the wet pink panties had raised her skirt to reveal the moist front of her wet pink panties. This time he ignored the calls of the guys in the boat and waded through the water towards her. Reaching out a hand and looking her in the eyes, he felt the front of her panties.

"Maybe you had better take them off to let them dry," he suggested.

"Maybe I should," she replied.

Within a few minutes they were back on the beach, which was unsuitably busy, and within a few minutes more they were locked in a cubicle in a nearby public toilet, taking off more than her wet pink panties.

It should have been everything that he had always assumed it would have been, but instead it was awkward, clumsy, and difficult.

"Not there," she said, "here." Trying to guide him.

"Sorry," he apologised.

"That's... no, it's slipped out again."

"It's kind of awkward in here."

"What if I..."

"No, that's even worse."

"How about this..."

"No, that's no better. What if I..."

"Ow. That hurts. Let me do it." She wiggled a little to the left, lifted one leg a little to the right.

"Yeah, that's it," he said; "now we're sailing... just a little more to the... OK... in we go... argh..." He came.

"Was that it?" she asked, failing to mask the dismay in her voice.

"Er... yes. Sorry," he said, embarrassed.

"Oh." She looked away, with a hint of a smirk on her lips.

It was the last thing she said as they dressed again in the cramped cubicle. Opened the door and were immediately arrested by the police officer called by an old lady who had listened to their exchange from the next cubicle.

In a short time they were taken away, booked in at the station, fingerprinted and locked in separate cells.

The Man Who Dreamt He Was Dreaming dreamt that he was dreaming that he was sitting disconsolate on a grey-blanketed bed in a grey cell. Dismayed, he lay back on the bed and closed his eyes.

"Just dream yourself back into another dream," he told himself. He relaxed his mind for a moment and then opened his eyes once more to find himself back in the house in which he had lived in the immediate time before **INTERFOLD**, with a very pale dark-haired girl kneeling on top of him wearing only a black bra and panties. Her face obscured by her wet hair as she stabbed him manically in the chest over and over and over again.

He woke with a jolt. It was dark. Gloomy and grey light hung heavy. The same room he had been in in the dream. There was an odd electric stillness around him.

"I'm still dreaming," he said aloud, recognising the unreality of the scene.

He dreamt himself settling back down into the bed. He dreamt himself closing his eyes. He dreamt himself dropping back down through layer upon layer of black sleep into a deeper layer of dreaming where he would look again for the girl in the wet pink panties, or some other missed opportunity to try to try again.

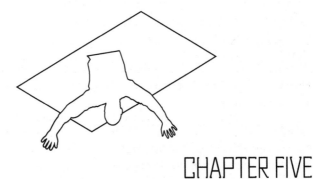

CHAPTER FIVE

1 Black McCarthy woke to the sound of the shower. He rolled onto his stomach, kept his eyes closed. Tried to enjoy the last few quiet moments of sleep before the day intruded. His thoughts switched back onto the search for Eugenides. If he could persuade Joylin to let him have access to the **INTERFOLD** Hotel register he might be able to locate the identity under which Eugenides was living in **INTERFOLD**. "I'll speak to her before I meet the Nurse with the Curse," he told himself. The Nurse with the Curse might also be able to help. His mind slipped across to the Nurse and a smile stirred on his face. He was looking forward to lunch already. He laughed once out loud. Smiled more broadly. Twisted suddenly onto his back and sat up, alarmed.

"Someone is in the shower," he said out loud.

"Of course there is someone in the shower," the Wolf

said, emerging from the shadow of the heavy hotel curtains, a cup of steaming black coffee in one hand. "Could you not tell from the rhythm of the water?"

Black stared at the Wolf in dismay. He had thought he would have more time before the Wolf returned.

"The question I ask myself, Wolf, is — who is in the shower?" Black said.

"I'd say that is self-explanatory," the Wolf answered, pulling a chair, with his free hand, up close to the bed where Black still sat. He gestured to the hotel uniform folded and draped carefully over an additional chair beside the closed door to the bathroom. Joylin's name badge was clearly visible, pinned to the lapel of her INTERFOLD uniform.

"But how did she get there?" Black asked, confused. His question was addressed to himself as much as to the Wolf, who had settled himself into the chair.

"My boy," the Wolf began, his voice weary with feigned exasperation, "that is a question you will have to answer for yourself."

Black dragged a hand through his sleep-styled hair. He hadn't had that much to drink the night before. At least he didn't think he had. He had never, as far as he could recall in any case, been both so drunk and yet so charming that he had managed to persuade a woman like Joylin to spend the night with him, yet not recollect a single detail of it happening. If it had happened it would have been be an event he would have wanted to remember.

"I haven't a clue," he said to the Wolf.

"McCarthy," the Wolf began, and Black knew it was bad if the Wolf was calling him McCarthy. "We are not paying you as handsomely as we are paying you to booze and shag your way through the women of Interfold." He paused as Black cringed. The Wolf was lowering his voice and speaking with quiet authority. It was a sign of displeasure. "We are paying you to find Eugenides."

"Wolf, I'm serious," Black said in his own defence. "I had a few beers last night with a guy who I think will prove very useful in locating Eugenides. Just a few beers, and I assure you that the girl in the shower may be in my shower, but she did not come back here with me last night and she did not spend the night in my bed."

"So how did she get into your shower, boy?" the Wolf asked, disbelieving.

"That is something you will have to ask her," Black said.

"Ask her?"

"Yep."

"Ha. Perhaps I shall, McCarthy. Perhaps I shall. But, before we are interrupted, what of Eugenides? Is he still here? Have you evidence of his presence? Or has he slipped away again? What news, McCarthy, what news?"

The telephone beside the bed rang, preventing Black from replying.

"Black McCarthy," he said into the phone.

"Black," said the voice of the Man Who Fell Through Floors, "it's me, Floors."

"Morning, Floors; can I call you back?"

"No need. Did you know we relocated again in the night?" Floors asked.

"No," Black said, taken aback. "Where?"

"Cambodia," Floors said.

"Cambodia," Black repeated.

"Cambodia," Floors said again. "Phnom Penh."

"Phnom Penh," Black said in alarm.

"Yeah, Phnom Penh," Floors echoed, "but that's not why I called."

"When?" Black interrupted before Floors could continue, ignoring the shaking head of the Wolf.

"When did I call? I'm calling you now. Black, I know Interfold time can be a little individual, but—"

"No. I mean 'when' as in 'what day, month, year in the history of the troubled nation of Cambodia have we relocated into?'"

"Ah. I see what you mean."

"Exactly."

"Oh, yes, I see indeed."

"So you take my point."

"I think I do."

"Khmer Rouge."

"Khmer Rouge."

"Killing Fields."

"Killing Fields."

"Genocidal communist madmen hell-bent on murdering Interfold-residing bourgeois dilettantes by their thousand."

"I'll call you back," Floors said and hung up immediately.

Black placed the receiver back in its cradle. He paused. The sound of the shower continued.

"Sorry about that, Wolf," Black said as the Wolf finished his coffee. "Where were we?"

"You were about to update me on your progress in seeking Eugenides."

"I was indeed, Wolf. As I was about to say before—"

The phone rang again. Black lifted the receiver to his ear.

"Me again," the Man Who Fell Through Floors said immediately. "February 1996."

"February 1996," Black repeated.

"February 1996," the Man Who Fell Through Floors echoed, "so all in all not too bad. A couple of Japanese business visitors were shot a week or two ago, but don't let that worry you. Interfold residents have diplomatic immunity."

"Does that stop you getting shot?" Black asked.

"As a rule," Floors assured him, "but that wasn't why I called."

"Why did you call?" Black asked.

"This," the Man Who Fell Through Floors said, and he fell through the ceiling of Black's room. He landed neatly to sit cross-legged on the end of Black's bed.

Black was speechless. Joylin was in the shower, although had no idea how or why. The Wolf was in his room demanding a report of progress, and now the Man Who Fell Through Floors was falling through floors at will and in particular through the floor that was above his ceiling and was now sitting on Black's bed looking rather pleased with himself.

Black had a feeling it was going to be a very long day.

2 The Man Who Lived in a Vacuum Cleaner woke in Alex's bed. He had slept very well indeed and felt refreshed. The Dwarf with the Horse and Pedro were nowhere to be seen. He lay on a plush white linen pillow and yawned.

Alex from Mars walked out of the bathroom with a too-small pink towel wrapped around her breasts, rubbing her long dark hair with another.

"Hi there, little man," she said, smiling at him. "How are you feeling this morning?"

"OK, I think," the Man Who Lived in a Vacuum Cleaner replied. He felt a little timid.

"Good," Alex said with a warm expression. She was

fascinated by the little man she had found floating in her drink and wanted him to feel at ease. "Would you like some breakfast? I ordered some coffee and pastries."

"Fantastic," he replied, leaping to his feet with enthusiasm. The surprisingly large penis flipped up to thud against his stomach and he realised he was still unclothed. He sat down again.

"Hey, don't worry about that," Alex reassured him. "You must have seen every inch of me last night."

Alex from Mars brought a tray over and placed it in the middle of the bed. On it sat a large plate of pains au chocolat, pains aux raisins and croissants, together with a pot of steaming coffee.

Alex hitched up her towel to allow herself to sit down on the bed. Shuffled around trying to get comfortable. Her towel fell open a little, revealing her left breast.

"What the hell," she said, throwing the towel on the floor and sitting cross-legged on the bed with the tray positioned between them. "Might as well just be comfortable. What would you like?"

"Pain aux raisins and coffee would be good," the Man Who Lived in a Vacuum Cleaner said, shuffling down the bed a little to sit opposite Alex. She broke a pastry into appropriately sized pieces and placed them on a plate before him. Poured some coffee into a cup.

"Sorry," she said, placing the large cup before him. "They weren't very helpful when I asked for a smaller cup."

"Don't worry," the Man Who Lived in a Vacuum Cleaner said. "I will just have to take care not to fall in." He stuffed a piece of pain aux raisins into his mouth and chewed. It was magnificent.

"So," Alex began, buttering a piece of croissant, "how did you come to be floating in a gin and tonic in the Red Light Basement?"

The Man Who Lived in a Vacuum Cleaner looked up at her. "I'm not sure I know," he said.

"So tell me what you do know," Alex said.

"The short version is that one day I shrank in the night. Woke the next day and found I was still shrinking. Some time later I was trapped in an industrial-grade vacuum cleaner until that bag lady found me and tried to eat me. One minute I was fighting for my life in her foul and festering mouth, the next I was flying through the air and landed in someone's gin.

Yours, I suppose. I don't remember another thing until I woke in your bag here last night."

"And who were you before you shrank?"

"Unhappy, mostly," he said.

"Unhappy?"

"Absolutely despairingly miserable."

"But you were here in Interfold?"

"For a little more than five years."

"Oh." Alex sipped her coffee. She wanted to ask where he had come from, but her knowledge of Earth geography had a habit of causing her embarrassment. She placed her cup back on the tray and spilt some coffee. Slipped off the bed to get a napkin to mop it up with.

"So where are you from?" the Man Who Lived in a Vacuum Cleaner asked.

"Mars," Alex replied.

"Of course you are," the Man Who Lived in a Vacuum Cleaner said, "and I am from Venus."

"Not with a penis like that," she said, regarding his surprisingly large penis.

"You mean..."

"Absolutely," Alex said, waggling a little finger at him.

"As small as that?"

"Complete Justins," she said.

"So, you really are from Mars?"

"Yes, I am."

"Wow." He was amazed. It was clear from her manner that she was telling the truth. "Mars, eh?"

"Yep, Mars, Red Planet, number four from the sun." Alex stood at the end of the bed with her legs slightly apart, her black and white striped delta pointing to the floor, hands on her hips. She was naked and breathtaking. The Man Who Lived in a Vacuum Cleaner felt faint.

"Alex..." the Man started to say, blinking hard as a wave of dizziness washed over him.

"Are you OK?"

"It's just..." he said, "that the problem with you being naked and... this..." — he gestured to the surprisingly large and painfully erect penis — "being so large is that the demand for blood down there is making me rather dizzy up here." He tapped the side of his head.

"I'm so sorry," Alex said, crawling onto the bed; "where are my manners?"

She pushed him down onto the bed. Pushed the breakfast tray aside and, taking the surprisingly large penis between her lips, introduced him to something known throughout the solar system as a Martian tongue-lashing.

3 Having left the room of Alex from Mars shortly after dawn, the Dwarf with the Horse was trying to find a way out of **INTERFOLD** — The Time Travel ~~Hotel~~ Republic. He was keen to resume their northerly migration and was unaware that **INTERFOLD** had twice relocated since he and Pedro had left the Red Light Basement the previous evening, or some years later as it now was.

"So go on," Pedro said with a grin to the little man walking by his side.

"Go on what?" the Dwarf replied, frowning. Every corridor looked the same to him and he had no idea how to get back to ground level without taking the stairs.

"Admit it," Pedro said.

"Admit what?"

"Admit that I was on fine form."

"When?"

"What do you mean, when?"

"I mean what I mean," the Dwarf said. "What are you on about?"

"What am *I* on about?"

"Yeah, what are you on about?"

"What am *I* on about?" Pedro shook his long black tail to emphasise his incredulity.

"What we need is an elevator," the Dwarf mused.

"Oh, that's right. Change the subject. Typical."

"Yep. An elevator." The Dwarf had no intention of repeating the Grand Hyatt incident.

"I am not going down the stairs," Pedro said.

"I am not asking you to."

"Not after the last time."

"I am not asking you to."

"It was humiliating. No stallion of my calibre should have to put up with that once, never mind twice."

"I am not asking you to," the Dwarf said again.

"I can never show my face in that resort again." Pedro shivered at the memory.

"Well, strictly speaking you shouldn't have shown your face there in the first place." The Dwarf chuckled.

"Are you laughing?" Pedro rolled his eyes in exasperation. "That's it, laugh at my misfortune."

"I wasn't laughing at you; I was remembering that little blonde."

"At the Grand Hyatt?"

"Yeah, at the Grand Hyatt," the Dwarf said.

Pedro thought for a moment. "Man, she was HOT!" he said.

"She was a little all right," the Dwarf agreed.

"She was on fire," Pedro said.

"She certainly was." The Dwarf chuckled again. "Remember how she kept squealing *Ride me Pedro, ride me*?"

"And she got what she asked for, all right." Pedro grinned. "A little bit of that old Spanish magic."

"Pity about the stairs, though." The Dwarf shook his head at the memory.

"I am not going down the stairs again, buddy," Pedro said, stopping and looking the Dwarf squarely in the eyes to make sure he knew he was serious.

"I am not asking you to," the Dwarf said again.

"You had better find the damn elevator."

"That's what I'm doing, Pedro. Cut me some slack here." The Dwarf shook his head.

"OK, OK, keep cool," Pedro said, flicking his tail.

They continued walking down the corridor as it curved away in front of them. Neither spoke as they scanned the walls in search of an elevator, finding only a sign for the stairs. Pedro ignored it and said, "You have to admit it, though."

"Admit what?" the Dwarf asked, shaking his head at the road ahead.

"Admit that I was on fine form," Pedro said.

"When?" the Dwarf asked, a sly smile on his lips.

4 Several hours earlier and many years later, somewhere between south-west England and Cambodia, the Bag

Lady Who Was Thrown Away woke in the INTERFOLD ER to find herself sharing a room with the Girl with Nine Lives. Refreshed by a good sleep and the thorough cleansing administered by a diligent Nurse with the Curse, she found herself looking at the new day and her roommate with a clarity of vision and mind which she had not experienced for some time.

She also found that, for the first time in many months, she could recall her reason for being in INTERFOLD — The Time Travel Hotel Republic. She groaned at the memory. Grimaced as she realised that she had wasted so much time. She had an assignment. She had to carry it out. She had to make up for the lost months, find the man she had been sent to seek and, she assumed, although her mind remained a little vague on this point, kill him.

"I am the Martian Assassin," she said softly to herself, remembering both her vocation and her planet of origin. She narrowed her eyes, hardened her resolve and got up out of the bed. Having wasted so much time, she needed to move quickly. The combination of hospitalisation and relocation held the potential for disaster and she could not let her true identity be discovered. She needed to get out of the ER and cover her tracks.

The Bag Lady/Assassin crossed the room and, standing beside the bed of the Girl with Nine Lives, she contemplated the sleeping girl's medical chart for a moment.

Having decided on her plan, she switched the medical chart of the Girl with Nine Lives with her own. Tiptoeing from the room, she left only the pair of red shoes that she had worn when disguised as the Bag Lady Who Was Thrown Away, and which the Nurse with the Curse had carefully placed under her bed, as a memento of her stay.

Once outside in a corridor the Bag Lady/Assassin realised she remained unclothed. This, she suspected, would be regarded as odd by anyone she happened to encounter, but in the absence of clothing there was little she could do about it and so she continued on her way out of the ER.

Clinging to the shadows, the Bag Lady/Assassin made her way along a series of dark and silent corridors and stairwells until she was a long way from the ER. Turning into one particularly well-lit corridor she was alarmed to hear giggling voices and running feet advancing towards her. She ducked back into the shadows and waited for them to pass.

By good fortune the running feet belonged to "The Feet of Dawn", INTERFOLD's classical Greece-inspired naked running team. They tore past the Martian Assassin wearing nothing more than running shoes on their feet and INTERFOLD ID pass cards on brightly coloured lanyards around their necks.

The Bag Lady/Assassin may have squandered a month or two blitzed out of her face from time to time, but she was a girl who knew good luck when it ran past her naked in the morning. As the last runner passed she slipped in and jogged along a pace or two behind, using their cover to carry her away into the depths of INTERFOLD. In her haste to run along with a convenient cover story failing to notice that with her long dark hair she was the only member of the team who was not blonde in every respect.

5 Back in Suite 9762 the Wolf was growling his displeasure at the sudden arrival of the Man Who Fell Through Floors.

"Damn it, McCarthy, we need to talk business," he hissed. "Get rid of him."

"OK, OK, keep calm, Wolf. I'll see what I can do," Black said. He went to persuade The Man Who Fell Through Floors to leave. "Listen, Floors," he began, "this is really not a good time."

"Is there someone in the shower?" the Man Who Fell Through Floors interrupted him.

"Yes," Black admitted with a furrowed brow, "there is someone in the shower, but—"

"You old dog," the Man Who Fell Through Floors said. "Not that one-legged dancer again?"

"No," Black said, "not the one-legged dancer again."

"Not the one-legged dancer?" the Man Who Fell Through Floors went on, enjoying the sport. "So who *did* you get lucky with?"

"I wouldn't necessarily call it *lucky*," Black said.

"Hey," the Man Who Fell Through Floors said with a sudden extra layer of curiosity clear in his voice, "it's not..."

"No, it is not," Black said.

"You don't know who I was going to say!"

"That may be. But it's not her."

"How do you know?"

"Believe me, it's not her."

"So who was I going to say?" the Man Who Fell Through Floors asked.

"Floors, buddy," Black said, "this really isn't a good time for me."

The Wolf growled a guttural *humph* of agreement.

"I was going to say the $10,000 Vagina," the Man Who Fell Through Floors said.

"The $10,000 Vagina?" Black asked, interested.

"The $10,000 Vagina," the Man Who Fell Through Floors said again.

"Who is she?" Black asked.

The Wolf threw his hands up in a gesture of disbelief and threw himself into a chair in a shadowed corner of Black's room.

"Don't mind me," he said, "you two carry on discussing pussy. I can wait. Really."

Taking him at his word, the Man Who Fell Through Floors started to tell Black McCarthy about the $10,000 Vagina, but at that moment the sound of the shower stopped. The Man Who Fell Through Floors looked at Black.

"So go on — who is she?" he asked.

"Shh," Black replied. "Quick. Hide in the shadows with the Wolf."

Floors stepped off the bed and stood behind the Wolf where he was barely visible. Black slipped out of bed and leant against the frame of the bathroom door, which was just open enough to send a long triangle of light into the room.

"How are you doing in there?" he asked without looking in.

"Don't come in," came an urgent reply.

"I wasn't going to come in," Black said. "Can I get you anything?"

"Don't come in," Joylin said again, not trusting Black to do as she asked.

"Don't worry. I am staying right here," Black said to reassure her, "although I am a little curious."

"Curious?"

"Curious."

"What about?" Joylin asked.

"Curious about you being in my bathroom."

"Don't come in," she said again in case he had forgotten.

"I wasn't going to come in," Black said. "I am going to wait just here, but I am still curious."

"Why are you so curious?"

"I am curious because you appear to be in my bathroom but your clothes appear to be out here..." He paused.

"Yes?"

"And I am wondering how you plan to become reacquainted with your clothes without coming out of the bathroom." He looked over to where the Wolf and the Man Who Fell Through Floors were hiding and raised his eyebrows with a smile, enjoying the sport.

"You could pass them in to me?" Joylin said.

"I could..." He paused again.

"But you're not going to?"

"I don't think so."

"Why not?" she asked.

"Put yourself in my position," Black said. "You have a, some might say, desirable yet feisty woman in your bathroom. You presume naked due to her clothes being out here on a chair. What would you do?"

"I would behave like a gentleman and pass the girl her clothes."

"But Joylin, you are assuming that I am a gentleman," Black said.

"Mr McCarthy," Joylin said in a familiar tone, "little though I know you, I know enough not to make that mistake. But I thought I should at least give you the opportunity to prove me wrong."

"Oh, Joylin, I am wounded."

"Yeah, yeah, yeah," she said, mocking him. "So what will it take?"

"What will it take?"

"Yes. What will it take?"

"For me to hand you in your clothes?" Black said.

"To hand me in my clothes."

"Hmm..." Black thought about it. "I don't know."

"You don't know?" she said, mocking him.

"Well, I—" Black began.

"And you claim that everyone has a price."

"I do indeed, Joylin," Black said. "A price and a vice. In this instance the former is front of mind, although the latter is not far behind."

"Really," she said as if uninterested.

"Really," Black continued. "You would like your clothes back, would you not?"

"I would."

"And you are currently naked?"

"I am."

"And those pink Interfold towels are remarkably small..."

"They are," she agreed.

"So to get your clothes you would need to come out here more or less naked and get them?"

"Yes, McCarthy—"

"Or else," he said, interrupting, "I could bring them in to you."

"Don't come in!"

"Or as a third option we could come to some agreement that would persuade me to hand them in to you."

"Some agreement?"

"Some... agreement," he said again.

"McCarthy," Joylin said, "can we get to whatever it is you are building up to?"

"Building up to?"

"Yes, McCarthy, get to the point if you have one."

"OK," he said, "here is the deal. Being a reasonable man, I am prepared to let you have your clothes back."

"You are?" Joylin asked, surprised and suspicious.

"I am."

"So what's the catch?"

"The catch?" Black said.

"The catch," Joylin confirmed.

"I am prepared to pass your clothes in to you if you come out here and get them."

"What?" Joylin asked, incredulous.

"I am prepared to pass your clothes in to you if you come out here and get them."

"Maybe I am being a little slow this morning, but what exactly is in that for me?"

"To put it simply, Joylin," Black said, with a note of victory in his voice and a wry look in the direction of the Wolf and the Man Who Fell Through Floors, "you will have to come out to find out."

6 The Man Who Lived in a Vacuum Cleaner regained consciousness to find Alex from Mars leaning over him with a measuring tape.

"What are you doing?" he asked in a whisper.

"I think it might pay to be scientific about this," Alex from Mars replied.

"What do you mean?" a confused Man Who Lived in a Vacuum Cleaner asked. "What happened?"

"Oh, I am sorry," Alex from Mars said, and she sat down beside him on the bed. "You passed out when you ejaculated. I suspect the blood supply to your head was a little restricted at that particular moment."

"I see," said The Man Who Lived in a Vacuum Cleaner, not seeing at all. "So why the tape measure?"

"Well," Alex began, frowning, "you have been out for about an hour..."

"Yes?"

"And in that time, I can't say for sure, but..."

"Yes?"

"I am sure you are bigger now than you were before." She shrugged.

"You don't mean..." the Man Who Lived in a Vacuum Cleaner began, looking down at the surprisingly large penis.

"Oh, no, no, no," Alex from Mars assured him, "I mean all of you. You look taller than before. I am sure you have grown."

"Grown?" the Man Who Lived in a Vacuum Cleaner asked, jumping up with his mind once more fully onboard. "Are you sure?"

"Yes," Alex from Mars said, "I am almost totally sure."

"Almost?" he asked. "Totally?" His shoulders dropped. "Are you sure?"

"Well..." Alex frowned. "I think so."

"How much?" he asked, looking himself over.

"I don't know exactly," Alex said, "which is why I was measuring you."

"Measuring me?"

"So that we can be sure."

"Sure?"

"Exactly. So that next time we can be sure."

"Next time?"

"Yes. Next time. It pays to be scientific about these things."

"Scientific?" he echoed, still not understanding.

"Yes, scientific," Alex explained, "so that next time we know exactly how much you have grown."

"Next time," he said, "scientific."

"That's it exactly," Alex from Mars said in encouragement. "Now, are you recovered enough?"

"Enough for what?" the Man Who Lived in a Vacuum Cleaner asked, wondering what she was on about.

"For this," Alex from Mars said. She pushed him gently back into a pillow, took the surprisingly large penis between her lips and dedicated her formidable tongue to science.

7 The Bag Lady/Assassin stayed with the Feet of Dawn as they completed their circuit and one by one began to peel off and head for home. Watching for her opening, the Bag Lady/Assassin picked a likely candidate whose stature was similar to her own and followed her from a good distance.

The girl, unaware that she was being followed, stopped outside her INTERFOLD apartment, pulled her pass card, which was on a chain around her neck, over her head and swiped it to open the door.

The kick that killed her was delivered with such speed and force that the girl would have had no idea that she was in danger before she was dispatched. The Bag Lady/Assassin calmly dragged the Girl with the Broken Neck through the open door by her hair and dumped the body on the floor in the hallway. She kicked the door closed behind her with the same lethal heel, switched on the lights and walked into the kitchen. She hoped the Girl with the Broken Neck kept a well-stocked refrigerator. All that running had made her hungry.

8 The Man Who Lived in a Vacuum Cleaner felt his way back to consciousness for the second time that morning. He felt a little nauseous but otherwise opened his eyes without too much trouble and fought to focus on the concerned face of Alex from Mars.

"Are you OK?" she asked.

"I think so," he said, trying to sit up.

"Hey, not so fast," Alex said. "That's twice today you've been out. Take it slowly."

"OK, did it work?" he asked with a note of hope in his voice.

"To the naked eye, I'd say yes."

"Are you sure?"

"You look a little bigger to me, but we said we would be scientific about this, so let me measure you to be precise." She took up her tape and measured the Man Who Lived in a Vacuum Cleaner. Frowned as she studied the result.

"So?" the Man Who Lived in a Vacuum Cleaner asked. "How did we do?"

"Not as well as I had hoped," Alex from Mars admitted, "but definite progress. You have grown almost half a centimetre."

"Only a half," he said with clear disappointment.

"I am afraid so."

"So how tall am I now?"

"A little over eight centimetres."

"Oh."

"But don't be too disheartened."

"It's hard not to be," he said.

"I know," she said, trying to sound reassuring, "but think it through. If you started out at, say, seven centimetres..."

"Yes."

"And we added another centimetre, then..."

"Yes."

"Well, that's two times per centimetre."

"Two times per centimetre," he echoed, seeing her point.

"So..."

"Yes?"

"But what if the growth increases proportionally as you get larger?"

"I see what you mean," he said as his optimism returned.

"How tall were you before you started shrinking?" Alex frowned as she considered the task.

"Six feet and six inches."

"Oh," she said, thinking the implications through. "What is that in centimetres?

"I was always told that was just under two metres."

"Oh."

"I know."

"So let's assume there is one metre ninety to go."

"OK."

"And that the growth will rise to an average of, say, one-point-five centimetres per time as we go on."

"So that would mean..." He frowned, calculating.

"Yes?"

"Only around another one hundred and twenty-five or so times to go before I get back to full height."

"Golly."

"I know." The Man Who Lived in a Vacuum Cleaner thought that that wouldn't necessarily be all that bad, although he hoped that he wouldn't pass out every time.

"I don't have any other plans," Alex from Mars said, "so if you are sufficiently recovered?"

"I think I am," the Man Who Lived in a Vacuum Cleaner replied, lying back with his arms behind his head.

"Then to work," Alex said, and down she went once more.

9   The Girl with the Broken Neck returned from the dead to find herself destined to regard life from a curious angle. The first curious thing she saw was a foraging stranger illuminated by the open door of her own INTERFOLD refrigerator, a cumbersome thing which although of high quality was only available in pink. Crouching as she drank from a carton of juice, the stranger presented the Girl with the Broken Neck with a view of such gynaecological detail that she immediately considered the stranger an intimate and greeted her accordingly.

"How are you getting on in there?" she asked the Bag Lady/Assassin.

The Bag Lady/Assassin turned around with ferocious velocity and hauled the Girl with the Broken Neck to her feet, staring hard into the girl's eyes, which wasn't easy given the jaunty angle at which the Girl with the Broken Neck was now wearing her head.

"You are alive," she said.

The Girl with the Broken Neck considered this statement and replied, "It certainly seems that way." She smiled what she considered a welcoming smile.

"But how can that be when your neck is quite clearly broken?"

"Oh, it's genetic," the Girl with the Broken Neck said, dismissing the subject with a wave of a hand. "Are you hungry?"

"Genetic?" the Bag Lady/Assassin echoed, preferring to

persist.

"It's a hereditary sort of thing," the Girl with the Broken Neck said. "We're all like it."

"All?"

"Yes, all of us," the Girl with the Broken Neck said, not wanting to elaborate. "How about I make us some breakfast and you can tell me what this is all about?"

"Who are *all of us*?" the Bag Lady/Assassin asked, unwilling to be distracted.

"Oh, that's not important," the Girl with the Broken Neck said. "I'll find you some clothes in a moment as well. Now, what can I get you? You look weak with hunger," — she looked The Bag Lady/Assassin up and down — "despite clear evidence to the contrary." She rubbed her broken neck and frowned.

The Bag Lady/Assassin stood silenced by the open familiarity of the girl whose neck she had broken. Her training told her to dispatch the Girl with the Broken Neck with all possible speed, but it seemed this would not be as simple as she had assumed. A large kitchen knife was at hand on a countertop, but this would be messy and the promised breakfast did appeal. Spilling blood on an empty stomach was never a joy.

"I'll kill her again after breakfast," she said to herself as the Girl with the Broken Neck cracked an egg into a sizzling pan

"How do you like your eggs?" she asked.

10 Black McCarthy and Joylin were in the corridor outside the closed door to Suite 9762. Joylin was dressing in a hurry while Black expressed remorse.

"I really am sorry, Joylin," he said. "I let things go a little too far."

"I'd say so, McCarthy."

"I only meant to have a little fun with you."

"At my expense, you mean," Joylin said.

"OK. I accept that is probably fair."

"Probably? McCarthy? Probably?"

"OK. Yes, you are right."

Joylin shook her head and buttoned her blouse. "And to

think I only came up here to help you out."

"Help me out?" Black asked, curious as to how.

"Yes, to help you out" — she paused — "and to use your shower."

"How were you going to help me out?" Black asked, hoping all was not lost.

"It's all right for you. Everything works up here. The plumbing on my level is abysmal. It's not all luxury in the Interfold Republic when no one else is picking up the tab for you, McCarthy. Some of us have to work for a living."

"In my defence, Joylin, I am here in the course of my work," Black said.

"Ha. Work," Joylin sneered. "And to think I only came up here to help you out."

"You said that," Black said, "but how exactly were you going to help me out?"

"What?" Joylin asked as if taken aback.

"You said you only came up here to help me out..." Black began.

"And to use your shower," Joylin said.

"Yes, and to use my shower. But I wondered how exactly?"

"How exactly?

"Yes," Black said, "how exactly?"

"I planned to use your shower in the normal way. To shower," Joylin said.

"No. You misunderstand," Black said. "I meant how exactly you were going to help me out?" He risked a smile in the hope that this would help. It didn't.

"You really are unbelievable. Do you know that, McCarthy?"

"Yes, Joylin," Black conceded.

"Do you really think that, after humiliating me as thoroughly as you have, I am still going to tell you exactly why I came up here this morning?"

"So you weren't here last night," Black said with relief. "I knew it."

"WHAT?" Joylin asked, clearly appalled anew.

"It's just good," Black said slowly, realising he had erred again, "to get confirmation."

"Confirmation." Joylin shook her head. "You really are the extreme, McCarthy, do you know that?"

"Yes, Joylin," Black said.

"And to think that I was starting to wonder whether I might be able to find you almost tolerable. Unbelievable.

It's bad enough that you assume that I would spend the night with you at all, never mind when you were clearly so drunk that you would have no hope of any recollection of it happening. Why I even considered helping you out I do not know." Joylin pulled on her skirt. "McCarthy, where are my shoes?"

"Don't worry, I'll find them," he said, and he quickly slipped back into Suite 9762. To his relief both the Wolf and the Man Who Fell Through Floors were nowhere to be seen. He retrieved Joylin's shoes and returned to the corridor.

"You realise you will have to kill them, don't you, McCarthy?" Joylin said as he handed her the shoes.

"What?" Black asked, alarmed. "Kill who?"

"Your two buddies. How else do you propose to restore my honour?"

"Your honour?" Black said.

"Yes, my honour."

"Your honour," Black said again. "Listen, Joylin. I am really sorry that I embarrassed you in there, but come on, no one saw all that much..."

"With towels as small as that," Joylin said.

"Even with towels as small as that. Come on, girl, be reasonable. You can't seriously expect me to restore your honour by killing two innocent bystanders to a harmless prank."

"I can and I do," Joylin said. "I demand justice and the restoration of my honour." She slipped into her shoes and pulled a very small pistol from the pocket of her jacket. "And this is the gun you are going to use to do the job."

Stung by the realisation that she was serious, Black stared at the gun.

"You cannot be serious, Joylin," he said as she placed the gun in his hand, taking no momentary joy from the brief touch of her skin on his own.

"I can and I am," she said, looking at her watch. "Now thanks to you I am late for work and you are late for your appointment with the Interfold Council."

"My what?" Black asked, thrown again.

"Oh, did I forget to mention it?" Joylin asked. "It must have been all the excitement of being humiliated. I completely forgot to tell you that you are summoned to present yourself to the Interfold Council this morning..." — she glanced at her watch again — "ten minutes ago."

"But what for?" Black asked.

"To paraphrase you, Mr McCarthy: you will have to put out to find out." She turned and started to walk away. Turned back to Black and added, "Take the red elevator from reception. Oh, and Black?"

"Yes, Joylin?" She had never called him Black before.

"Don't forget to kill your friends for me."

Black stared at her back as she walked away, completely lost for words.

11 Joylin turned a corner and stopped. Ran a hand through her hair and exhaled.

"How did it go?" the Wolf asked as he materialised out of the wall at her side.

"He took the gun."

"Good work, Joylin. Good work. And he is to see the Council?"

"This morning."

"Well," the Wolf said, "there is nothing we can do about that. Just keep close to him and make sure that we know whatever he knows before he knows he knows it."

"That," Joylin said with a smile, "won't be difficult."

CHAPTER SIX

The Man Who Dreamt He Was Dreaming was dreaming he was dreaming. He remained asleep week after week, and although the time he reclined rose and fell with the **INTERFOLD** tide, the sum of the stream in which he dreamed was a considerable measure in anybody's scheme.

Through dream layer upon dream layer he dreamt he was dreaming. He was searching for the girl in the wet pink panties, but she was rarely where he wanted her to be and never alone. There was always another man at her side, always some chancer, some hoper, some lower being blocking his path.

In an attempt to elude the fools, the Man Who Dreamt He Was Dreaming dreamt himself high on a Welsh mountainside. In a hamlet comprising a pub, a post office and a converted barn, owned by the landlord of the pub, which served as a dormitory for hikers.

He dreamt the scene vivid and real. The girl in the wet

pink panties was changing after a hike, removing clothes wet from crossing a stream. With her back to the Man Who Dreamt He Was Dreaming she sat wearing only pink panties, which he was reassured to see were damp. He could see a glimpse of the edge of the swell of her considerable breasts only metres away, but beyond her was the usual other rolling his ridiculous eyes, taunting him with the knowledge that he, though a fool, had a full view of that which the Man Who Dreamt He Was Dreaming was denied.

The Man Who Dreamt He Was Dreaming considered a mad rush to take in the full view, but instead turned away disconsolate and descended the stairs to the lower room, which contained little apart from a large table cluttered with empty bottles and a wood burner unnecessary in the temperate climate of his dreams.

A thin red-haired girl wearing a white T-shirt and a blue miniskirt sat at the table.

"Hi," she said, crossing her legs and smoking a cigarette.

"Hi," the Man Who Dreamt He Was Dreaming said in reply, looking at her face. Her eyes were made up with heavily defined eyeliner marks, which he found familiar. She smiled in response to his studying her eyes. Deciding that he needed a drink even if this was a dream, he began checking the bottles that crowded the table.

"They're all empty," the Thin Red Girl said. "I've already checked."

"That's a pity," the Man Who Dreamt He Was Dreaming said. "Is the pub still open?"

"No. Not today. Have they got anything to drink up there?" She signalled upwards with the cigarette.

"Not that I know of."

"Shall I ask them?"

"It can't do any harm."

"You don't sound too sure," the Thin Red Girl said.

"Maybe I'm not."

"Maybe you're not?"

"Maybe I'm not."

"What is there to be unsure about? We are down here without a drink and they are up, either with or without a drink. Something I can clarify by asking."

"Ignore me," he said. "Go and ask them."

"I will," the Thin Red Girl said. She uncrossed her legs and stood up. "Here, hold this." She handed him the cigarette and ascended the stairs halfway so that only the very short skirt and her long thin pale legs were visible. He traced their lines with his eyes from her ankles to the point where her thighs disappeared underneath the blue skirt.

The Thin Red Girl turned round and crouched down enough to lower her head below ceiling level.

"I don't think now would be a good time," she said. A moan that might have been a whimper drifted to his ears.

"It seems not," he said.

"Are you looking up my skirt?" the Thin Red Girl asked.

The Man Who Dreamt He Was Dreaming considered the question. It was his dream, after all, and so he answered, "Yes. Yes, I am." He glanced up her skirt again just to emphasise the point.

"Oh," she said, "I thought you were. So what colour are they?"

"What colour?"

"Yes. What colour are my knickers?"

"I couldn't see," he admitted.

She descended a few steps but remained positioned above him. "Would you like to?"

He considered his response. "Yes," he said.

"Guess first," the Thin Red Girl said.

"Guess?" he said.

"Yes. Guess what colour my knickers are. I bet you can't."

"Black?" he said.

"No."

"White?"

"Uh-uh."

"Red?"

She shook her head.

"Blue?"

"No."

"Yellow?"

"No."

"Pink?"

"Not even close."

He thought for a minute. "Polka dots?"

"No."

"Stripes."

"No."

"Green?"

"With this hair colour? Please!"

"Well, I really don't know," he said with a shrug of defeat.

"I suppose you want me to show you," she said, smiling.

"Yes, I do," he said, reasoning that since this was his dream there was no point hanging around.

"Well, I can't," she said.

"You can't?" he asked, disappointed and suspecting an all-too-familiar course of events was about to unfold.

"No," she said, "I can't."

"Why not?" he asked.

"Think about it," she said, holding eye contact to emphasise her point.

"Think about it?"

"Yes. Think about it," she said again.

"I am," he said.

"It is really very obvious," she said, placing a hand on each thigh.

"Is it?" he asked, thinking it over.

"Oh yes."

He thought it over. "Obvious?" he said, unable to think any further.

"Yes," she said softly. "Really. Very. Obvious."

"Show me," he said, almost a whisper.

"I suppose I could," she agreed, "just show you..." and she began to lift her skirt slowly, "a glimpse." She pushed the fabric of the skirt a little higher and eased her legs a little apart.

He took a step towards her and, holding eye contact, placed a hand on a thigh and moved it slowly up until his fingers made contact. She closed her eyes as he stroked and probed. Slumped against his shoulder. Wrapped her arms around him and kissed his neck.

Oh my God, he said silently in his head, *it's an absolute thicket!* He probed and stroked. Stroked and probed but could not penetrate her thick curls. Soft though they were, they appeared to form an impenetrable fortress and no matter how hard he pressed and tried he simply could not get inside.

This appeared to have no effect of restraint on the Thin Red Girl who kissed him ever more frantically and tightened her grip, throwing her legs around his waist, sending him off-balance. He fell back against the table, sending bottles crashing. He manoeuvred them both onto the bench beside the table, still pushing and probing with his hand. He leant against the back of the bench but it gave way with a crack, throwing him backwards. He threw both arms out to steady himself and the Thin Red Girl flailed back herself and fell off him as he tumbled over through the broken back of the bench, and straight through the solid stone wall behind.

He found himself suddenly on the floor of a dark room, positioned between a flickering detuned analogue TV and a slumbering man of huge proportions wearing thick black-rimmed glasses which reflected the fizzing transmission of the TV back on itself. The Thin Red Girl had disappeared.

"Bollocks," he said. "Bollocks. Bollocks. Bollocks." He kicked the fat sleeper, who grunted but stirred no further.

The Man Who Dreamt He Was Dreaming looked at the wall through which he had entered the room. Solid. Unbreachable. He ran a hand over the perfect plaster. "Sod it," he said out loud, and he walked out of the room and out of the house.

He closed the door behind him and found himself outside an average terrace house on an average-income housing estate in Basildon in 1986. A young man with a familiar face was urinating in the front garden of the house next door where a party was in progress. Otherwise all was quiet under the amber light of street lamps.

The Man Who Dreamt He Was Dreaming realised that he was still holding the cigarette the Thin Red Girl had handed him. He looked at the red ring of lipstick around the tip and threw it away. Put his hands into pockets and walked slowly away.

"At least I didn't get stabbed this time," he said.

"Don't be so sure," a voice said behind him. He turned a sharp about-face and received a punch that knocked him back onto the ground. A girl with long dark hair and black underwear jumped down upon him and began stabbing him manically again and again and again.

The Man Who Dreamt He Was Dreaming recalled that the girl's hair was quite wet as he sat up with a shudder. The room about him sat languid in the dull familiar light of his in-between dream.

He slumped back on to the bed. Threw himself onto his side. Pulled the covers over his head and, familiar by now with the procedure, succumbed once more to a dream of a dream.

CHAPTER SEVEN

1 The Dwarf with the Horse and Pedro were having a bad morning. Not only had they been forced to take the stairs, having failed to locate an elevator, but they had been arrested by a squad of **ASSIIR** (Agency for State Security and Intelligence of the **INTERFOLD** Republic) agents.

It was an unpleasant experience for everyone involved. For the Dwarf with the Horse and Pedro because they had been apprehended in **INTERFOLD** without permits or ID, and with a large unpaid tab at the Red Light Basement. For the agents because Pedro and the Dwarf had resorted to the use of the stairs in an attempt to evade detention, despite the unpleasant precedent of the Grand Hyatt incident.

One agent in particular had caught the full backdraft of Pedro's fear in descent. Given Pedro's level of consumption of beer the previous evening, the timing of the agent in chasing Pedro down a stairwell had been unwise. Attempting to jump onto Pedro's back, foolhardy. Being in the way when hooves were slipping, knees were buckling and internal controls were giving way, a cause of mirth for the Dwarf. Mirth that continued to arise occasionally even post-arrest.

"That's it! Laugh at my misfortune," Pedro said in disgust.

"I'm not laughing at you," the Dwarf assured him.

"It's always the same with you humans," Pedro continued. "Pick on the easy target. I told you I didn't want to go down the stairs, but can you find another way out? Oh, no. Typical."

"I am not laughing at you, Pedro," the Dwarf said again. "I am laughing at him." He pointed at the unfortunate ASSIIR agent who looked terrible and smelt even worse.

"Just deserts," Pedro snapped, flicking his mane. "Pedro does the riding. No one rides Pedro."

"Especially not on the stairs," the Dwarf said.

"What do you expect? I AM A HORSE," Pedro shouted.

"Keep it down, horse," the leading ASSIIR agent said in a flat monotone.

"Listen to old no-balls," the Dwarf said in a low voice. During the fracas of their arrest the Dwarf had attacked the lead ASSIIR agent with a violent series of headbutts to the groin, only to discover what any long-term INTERFOLD resident could have told him. The ASSIIR agents were, are and may well continue to be eunuchs.

"You wouldn't guess it from his voice," Pedro said. "You would expect him to be all squeaky."

"Like a little girl."

"On helium."

"Like the redhead in Riga. Remember her?" the Dwarf asked.

"The ice-skating ballet dancer with the piercing?"

"That's the one."

"How could I forget?"

"I said keep it down. Prisoners are not permitted to discuss sexual conquests," the lead ASSIIR agent said again, waving his gun at the Dwarf to emphasise his point.

"Where are you taking us anyway?" the Dwarf asked him.

"You are to appear before the Interfold Council."

"What for?" Pedro asked.

"You do not have a residency or visitor permit and are in possession of an unlicensed animal," the most fragrant of three ASSIIR agents said to the Dwarf.

"Looks like I'm in the clear," Pedro said.

"Don't bank on it," the Dwarf replied.

"The Council sits in an emergency session the morning after every relocation to consider in sequence and concurrently any immigration anomalies resulting from the change in time and place. Their decision is final and binding. There is no appeal system and sentencing is implemented with immediate effect," the third ASSIIR agent said in a voice as flat and monotonous as his colleagues'.

"Relocation?" Pedro said to the Dwarf. "Immigration?"

"Not a clue," the Dwarf said. "I thought it was a new hotel resort we had missed."

"You are illegally present in the Interfold Republic," the lead ASSIIR agent said to the Dwarf. "The Council does not encourage illegality and takes a very hard line in dealing with transgressors to discourage those who would exploit the relocation tendency of the Interfold Republic in this way."

"I suppose there is no chance of stopping off for a beer on the way?" the Dwarf asked.

"Your supposition is correct."

"Guessed as much," the Dwarf said to Pedro.

"How about breakfast?" Pedro asked.

"No," ASSIIR Agent 2 said to the Dwarf.

"Coffee?" the Dwarf suggested.

"Shut up and walk."

"Tea it is, then," Pedro said to the Dwarf with a wink, as they continued to be led at gunpoint to their appearance before the Council.

2 The Girl with Nine Lives had also been introduced to a triumvirate of ASSIIR agents over breakfast that morning, having regained consciousness. Doctor Klown had attempted to explain that she was a long-standing resident, but the chart on the end of her bed said otherwise.

"Doctor," the lead ASSIIR agent said, "we have to arrest her. You know the rules."

"But there has been a mistake."

"That is not my concern."

"I assure you there was another patient here last night and the charts and ID verification have been switched. It's a simple administrative error."

The three ASSIIR agents looked around the room in perfect unison.

"So where is the other patient now?" Number 2 asked.

"Where? Well, I don't... that is..." Doctor Klown said.

"Unless you can produce a second patient, Doctor, we are going to arrest the one we have."

"I understand that. But I can personally vouch for her identity."

"Doctor," ASSIIR Agent 3 said, "you know as well as I do that your word carries no weight in Interfold law without documentary evidence in support."

"I am sure she can obtain some ID if you will let her return home to retrieve it."

"No way," the Girl with Nine Lives said.

"Why not?" a confused Doctor Klown asked.

"It's personal, Doctor."

"In any case it is not permitted," the lead ASSIIR agent said. "Interfold state regulations require ID and permits to be carried at all times. If your patient has neither and you cannot produce them on her behalf then we are required to present her to the Interfold Council without delay. Is your patient fit to move?"

"Well, she has had a very bad fall. Ordinarily I would want to keep her under observation..." Doctor Klown began.

"I'm fine," the Girl with Nine Lives cut in.

"I think you should let me be the judge of that," the doctor said, blushing.

"Really, Doctor, you are sweet, but you know as well as I do that there is nothing wrong with me."

"I really think you should leave this to me," Doctor Klown said, attempting to position himself as a voice of authority.

The Girl with Nine Lives brushed this aside. "Don't be silly, Doctor," she said. "Now, where are my clothes," — she lifted the sheets a little and peered underneath — "since I don't appear to be wearing any?"

Doctor Klown leant closer and whispered, "I don't think you fully appreciate the gravity of the situation. The Council is notoriously merciless in deciding immigration issues."

"I am not afraid of the Council."

"Perhaps you should be."

"Should I?"

"I think you should. Their reputation is far from compassionate."

"I have no need for compassion and I am not entirely without connections."

"At least let me accompany you. There may be something I can do," Doctor Klown said. He had no idea what, but he felt responsible and compelled not to let the Girl with Nine Lives from his sight.

"You are very sweet. If they will permit it, then OK."

"Is that OK? I can accompany her?" Doctor Klown asked the lead ASSIIR agent.

"You may," he replied.

"Good," Doctor Klown said. "That's that, then. Shall we get on our way?" He looked expectantly at the Girl with Nine Lives, who remained in bed holding a sheet up over her chest.

"One small thing, Doctor," she said.

"Yes?"

"My clothes?"

"Ah, bit of a problem there," he explained.

"In what way?" the Girl with Nine Lives asked.

"We had to cut them off you last night."

"Cut them off me?"

"Cut them off you."

"Whatever for?"

"They were soaked in blood," he explained. "We had to be sure you were not seriously injured."

"So what do you suggest?" she asked. "I can't very well appear before the Council naked."

"It makes no difference to us," the second ASSIIR agent said.

"That goes without saying!" the Girl with Nine Lives said with disdain.

"We can take you as you are," the third ASSIIR agent said, stepping forward, his face grey with sudden aggression. "I can assure you it will not embarrass us, although the Council may frown upon such behaviour."

"Perhaps I can find something for you to wear," Doctor Klown offered, looking around without inspiration.

"Perhaps some of those surgical pyjamas?" the Girl with Nine Lives suggested.

"Of course!" Doctor Klown said. "What a good idea." He stood smiling at the Girl.

"So..."

"Ah, yes." He coughed. "Straight away." He strode from the room. Leaving the Girl with Nine Lives and the three eunuchs in awkward silence.

"Going anywhere nice for your holidays this year?" she asked.

The three ASSIIR agents ignored her.

"Thought not," the Girl with Nine Lives said to herself with a hint of satisfaction in her smile.

3 Black McCarthy was pacing the corridor outside the official chamber of the INTERFOLD Council. A series of ASSIIR triumvirates and captives had arrived and entered the chamber, but every time he enquired as to when he would be seen he was simply told to wait.

"Had you been here when required, you would have been seen immediately. Really, Mr McCarthy, you cannot expect the exalted Interfold Council to drop important business just because you have finally found time in your schedule to turn up," he had been told by an unhelpful clerk who he thought would have been cute had it not been for her frosty manner.

"I had no idea anyone wanted to see me. I came immediately when I became aware," he explained.

"Save it for the Council," she had replied, holding up an abrupt palm before disappearing inside the chamber once more, leaving Black alone in the corridor.

"Not been called in yet?" the Wolf enquired, materialising beside him.

"No," Black replied.

"Hmmm." The Wolf mused. "Most inconvenient."

"Indeed," Black mumbled.

"What?" the Wolf asked.

"I said *indeed*," Black said.

"Oh," the Wolf said. "So what about Eugenides? I did not get a chance to hear your report." He looked at Black.

"There is not much to report," Black admitted.

"Huh." The Wolf considered McCarthy's odd Converses, the left one red, the right one green. "Oh, well. Keep at it. Time is money and all that, McCarthy, grains of sand. This fellow needs locating."

Black considered his own palm for a moment. "You could give me a little more to go on, you know."

"Could I?"

"Yes, you could. The brief is a little light on direction, you know, Wolf."

"That's the way of things, McCarthy, old boy. If it was easy it would hardly be worth my paying you, would it?"

"I suppose not. But you could give me a little more to go on, just the same."

"No. I cannot," the Wolf said, stretching to his full height and looking down at McCarthy. "To do so would put you in greater danger."

"I wasn't aware I was in any danger," Black retorted.

"Don't be naïve, Black," the Wolf said. "As I said, I do not want to put you in greater danger than necessary. It is better that you work blindly, less likely to arouse unwelcome suspicion." He paused. "Also..."

"Yes?"

"To tell you more would break the agreement we have with the insider who led us to Interfold."

"You received information from an Interfold insider?"

"We did. But although our would-be ally was prepared to give us limited information, they insisted on some restrictive terms of engagement."

"We have an ally?"

"You do not," the Wolf admonished him with a raised finger of warning.

"But you do?" Black asked.

"To a degree, that is correct."

"Why do I get the feeling that I am just a pawn in the game? A necessary but expendable foot soldier?"

"Because in a sense you are," the Wolf said.

"In a sense?"

"Yes. In a sense."

"Care to expand on that a little?" Black asked.

"No."

"No?"

"Yes. No."

"Not at all?" Black stared at the Wolf.

"No."

"Come on, Wolf, give me a little more to work with here!" Black dragged a hand through his hair. Shook his head. Looked up at the ceiling. "You have given me next to nothing to work with and yet here you are in Interfold checking up on me, expecting results inside a week. If you have more information, let me have enough to have a fighting chance of success."

The Wolf considered Black's shoes again for a moment before replying. "OK."

"OK?"

"OK," the Wolf repeated. "But subject to all the usual caveats."

"The usual caveats?"

"Yes. For the sake of good order."

"For the sake of good order?"

"Of course."

"What does that mean?" Black asked.

"It means what it means, McCarthy."

"Wolf. Had it not been that I was not entirely with you to start with, I would be in danger of losing the thread of your point."

"That was partly my intention."

Black stared at the Wolf. "Partly your intention," he repeated.

"Yes."

Black walked several paces away. Stopped and thought for a moment. Turned and raised a finger, ready to speak, but then changed his mind. The Wolf waited. Black turned away again and after a moment said without turning, "So, to recap..."

"Yes?"

"I am in a sense a foot soldier; you have more information but you cannot reveal it, or rather you will enlarge to a degree but only subject to all the usual caveats for the sake of good order. Does that sum it up?"

"Quite concisely, McCarthy. Well done."

"So?"

"So what?"

"So are you going to give me a little more information or not, Wolf?"

"No," the Wolf said, holding an urgent finger aloft. Head cocked, he listened to a sudden and unseen distraction and then simply disappeared, leaving Black dismayed.

"Thanks," he said aloud.

"That's OK," the Wolf said, reappearing. "Sorry that took so long. Now, what were we talking about?"

"It was only a second ago, Wolf; surely you remember?"

"Seconds to you; three weeks, two days to me, McCarthy. General hints or a brief summary, perhaps. Come on, boy, I have a recollection that this was important."

"You were offering to give me a little more information to work with in finding Eugenides."

"Was I?" the Wolf asked, incredulous. "Are you sure, boy? Sounds a little out of character, wouldn't you say?"

"Well, I... couldn't say, Wolf, but you have to admit the information I have is thin. You could usefully give me a little more information, you know. Perhaps something gleaned from your Interfold insider?" Black chanced his arm.

"Who told you about that?" the Wolf asked, alarmed.

"You did, Wolf," Black assured him. "You did."

"Humn. Did I? What was I thinking?" The Wolf mused to himself for a moment. "Oh, well. What do you want to know, McCarthy?"

"Anything that would be useful, Wolf, anything that would be useful," Black said, suspecting he would receive exactly the opposite.

"There is little that I can tell you, McCarthy. We may well have been meticulously misled thus far. To tell you what little more we have may mislead you further and endanger the entire mission."

"Misled?" Black asked.

"Misled indeed," the Wolf assured him. "Up the garden path and round the houses with crimson fish."

"Who by?" Black asked.

"By my erstwhile ally on the Interfold Council," the Wolf said.

"On the Council?" Black asked, surprised.

"Yes, on the Council," the Wolf repeated. "Do try and keep up, boy."

"Of course, Wolf," Black said, a little put out.

"Good good. As I was saying, the danger is that my ally may well turn out to be nothing of the sort."

"Your ally?" Black asked.

"Yes, my ally," the Wolf said.

"On the Interfold Council."

"Yes, on the Interfold Council, McCarthy; I thought we had established that!"

"So how do we find out whether this ally has misled us?" Black asked.

"How, McCarthy?" the Wolf asked. "By finding Eugenides, of course."

"Of course."

"So there you are. Best I can do." The Wolf contemplated

Black. "Best I leave you to it, McCarthy." He slapped Black on the shoulder and strode purposefully into the shadows and disappeared.

Finding himself standing alone with nothing more to guide him at the end of their conversation than at the beginning, Black pulled a packet of Gitanes from the pocket of his pin-striped jacket. He stared at the remarkable blue and white box with curiosity. He did not smoke and had no idea how it had come to be in his pocket. Nevertheless he pulled a Gitane from the packet and placed it between his lips. A further exploration into his jacket pocket produced a book of RLB matches; he struck one red tip and lit the Gitane and puffed out a cloud of satisfying blue smoke.

4 "Smoking is not allowed!" a chorus of high-pitched ASSIIR agents squealed at Black.

"They really are a tiresome lot," the Girl with Nine Lives said.

"Who are they?" Black asked.

"For the most part little more than a genderless annoyance," she replied, "and the guardians of law and order in Interfold." She waved a dismissive hand.

"Ah. Guess I had better put this out, then," Black said. "Not that I actually smoke. They just happened to be in my pocket, so..."

"That sounds as lame as every other story we have heard this morning," a humourless ASSIIR agent said to Black, his purpose to annoy the Girl with Nine Lives.

"Ignore his tone," the Girl advised Black. "They are misogynists of some renown."

"Do you work in the ER?" Black enquired.

"Do I work in the ER?"

"Yes. Do you work in the ER?" Black confirmed.

"What in Interfold makes you ask that?" the Girl with Nine Lives asked with a frown.

"You are wearing surgical pyjamas?" Black suggested.

"What, these? I assure you this is a result of a very inconvenient identity theft, of which I am of course the *victim*," she emphasised for the benefit of her guards, "rather than the perpetrator."

"Identity theft?" Black asked, bemused.

"Yes, identity theft. It is increasingly common in Interfold as aliens attempt to avoid the pitfalls of the relocation tendency. It is far simpler to steal the identity of a true Interfolder than risk being hauled in front of the council and their somewhat eccentric approach to justice." She looked Black up and down. "But I take it you are not an Interfolder yourself?"

"No," Black said. "I am only here temporarily, but legally so. I assume I have been summoned to discuss the terms of my remaining." He looked into the inquisitive blue eyes of the Girl with Nine Lives and wondered if she might be of use in his search for Eugenides, reluctant though he was to raise the subject in the presence of the ASSIIR agents. "Who exactly are these guys?" he asked.

"This lot?" she replied with disdain. "They are a ball-less disgrace to Interfold. Officially they are ASSIIR agents. ASSIIR: Agents for State Security and Intelligence in the Interfold Republic. They aspire to be something along the lines of East Germany's Stasi, but mercifully they are significantly more incompetent. They can be a real pain if you are caught without ID post-relocation, as I was myself just this morning. What about you, Mr...?"

"McCarthy. Black McCarthy." He offered a hand, which she gave a firm and proper handshake.

"Mr McCarthy," she said in formal confirmation. "What brings you to Interfold?"

"I am looking for someone," he said.

"Oh, really?" the Girl with Nine Lives asked. "Anyone in particular?"

"Yes," Black confirmed. "Someone who does not want to be found."

"How exciting," the Girl said with genuine interest. "How are you getting on?"

"Not so well," Black admitted. "To be honest I am not even sure he is still in Interfold. If he is, either he must be in hiding under an assumed or stolen name or the name I was originally given was false. The problem is that, apart from his potentially false name, I do not have a whole lot to go on. Progress is therefore rather slow." *No surprise given that you haven't exactly focused on the problem, though, old boy*, he added to himself.

"How intriguing," the Girl said. "I would be glad to assist

in any way I can once this morning's inconvenience is out of the way, of course. I have been in Interfold since before the declaration of independence, so if you need a guide to our wayward republic I shall be happy to help you in any way I can."

"Thank you," Black said, surprised. "That really is very kind of you."

"Not at all," she said. "You seem like a decent enough chap. The majority would not have even spoken to me whilst I was in the custody of these three, and in any case you have helped distract me from my predicament. Oh, good, here comes the doctor," she added as Doctor Klown arrived.

"Hey, Doc," Black said by way of a greeting.

"Oh," Doctor Klown said, his enthusiasm quite absent. "You again."

"Oh, good, you know Mr McCarthy already. Excellent. Doctor, I was just offering to do all I could to assist Mr McCarthy in his hunt for..." She paused. "What did you say his name was?"

"Eugenides," Black said.

"Oh, I say!" the Girl with Nine Lives exclaimed, taken aback. "Now, why is that name so very familiar?" She paced away a few metres, one arm folded across her body, tapping her chin with one elegant index finger. "Think, think, think. I know that name, Mr McCarthy, and give me time and I will remember why. I genuinely do think that I will be able to help you here, mark my words."

"Do you really think that is wise?" a concerned Doctor Klown asked. "Given the circumstances the best policy would be to keep a low profile and leave Mr McCarthy to his own methods. You don't know what the Council has planned for either him or you. No point risking their ire unnecessarily."

"Oh, Doctor, you are such a sweetie to be so concerned for my welfare, but I assure you I am a girl who can find her own way home. Please do not worry unduly on my behalf. You have been too kind already in simply accompanying me to the Council hearing."

"Hmm. Well. OK, it is your decision," Doctor Klown said, steering The Girl with Nine Lives a few steps away from Black before whispering, "but really you know nothing of this man. I can only urge caution."

"I promise I will keep that in mind," she whispered in reply, smiling at Black.

Black smiled back, thinking, *You never know; this could be a real breakthrough*. But before he could open up a further line of enquiry the Clerk Who Would Have Been Cute Were She Not So Frosty returned.

"The Council are ready to see her," she said to the ASSIIR agents, "and you, Mr McCarthy, are to come with me." She turned and strode away along the corridor.

"Best of luck," Black said to the Girl with Nine Lives, and with a cursory nod to Doctor Klown he followed the frosty yet cute clerk.

5   The Dwarf with the Horse and Pedro were pleading their case before the INTERFOLD Council or rather, to be precise, before the lone council member who had been delegated to deal with that morning's crop of relocation offenders. She was tall and imperious, wearing a smart and official-looking red uniform business suit of jacket and knee-length skirt. Her face was disguised, as INTERFOLD custom decreed, by a plain white mask and she wore a red bowler hat. She paced constantly back and forth, firing questions at the Dwarf and his fine Spanish companion. Questions that Pedro, as the more eloquent partner, was having increasing trouble answering.

"It is all a terrible misunderstanding," he pleaded. "An innocent mistake anyone could have made. We had no idea this was a restricted area."

"So you admit you entered Interfold illegally?" she argued.

"Not as such," Pedro said. "You must understand we have no idea what Interfold *is*."

"You really don't expect me to believe that, do you? No idea what the Interfold Republic *is*?" She stamped a heel, incredulous and impatient. "Enough of this nonsense. Tell me the truth. Who sent you? On whose orders did you illegally infiltrate Interfold? Who gave you refuge during your time here? Who are you working for?"

"If I could just confer with my associate for a moment," Pedro said with a polite horse smile.

"What is she on about?" the Dwarf whispered, peering over his shades at the pacing interrogator.

"Not a clue," Pedro replied to his diminutive associate

whilst continuing to smile broadly at the woman. "What do you think we should do?"

"No idea," the Dwarf said.

"I could... you know," Pedro suggested.

"No, Pedro. I think that will only make matters worse."

"It has got us out of a tight spot before."

"Maybe, but not as often as it has got us into a tight spot in the first place!" The Dwarf looked at Pedro over the top of his shades.

Pedro chuckled. "It's that old Spanish magic," he said. "The ladies just don't know how to say no. You never know, though; she looks a little tense but maybe she's an equestrian kind of girl on the quiet?"

"I have my doubts," the Dwarf said, sceptical.

"Have I ever let you down?" Pedro asked.

"Well, there was that occasion in Helsinki in '89."

"Helsinki?"

"Yes. Helsinki."

"Finland?"

"Yep. Finland."

"Did I?" Pedro asked. "I don't recall. What happened?"

"You don't remember?"

"Not a thing."

"Nothing at all?" the Dwarf asked.

"Nothing at all," Pedro confirmed apologetically.

"I don't believe it!"

"Sorry," Pedro said. "But I don't remember a thing after we went into that sauna with the three girls from the army."

"How could you forget?" the Dwarf asked.

"Well, you know me and spirits. All that vodka..."

"Exactly my point!" the Dwarf exclaimed, exasperated. "Once you passed out they lost interest. I couldn't take three of them on by myself."

"Hey, buddy. I had no idea. I'm really sorry. I know how much you like the army chicks."

"What a missed opportunity!" the Dwarf said.

"So what about it?" Pedro asked, tipping an ear in the direction of their tormentor.

"I don't know."

"It has to be worth a shot," Pedro pleaded.

"OK, but if it makes things worse you are going to owe me big time, buddy."

"OK, OK. Don't worry; I'll be as persuasive as I can," he

assured his diminutive companion before turning his attention back to the prosecutor. He explained once more that it was all a terrible misunderstanding that they of course regretted enormously, and had they only realised they would have changed course and gone elsewhere. All this was accompanied with a flash of charming smile here, a considered flick of the tail there, a wink of an eye and a flex of a powerful flank. As a finale Pedro very briefly allowed the full length of his considerable appendage to extend before retracting it immediately in the hope that it would tease, tempt and perhaps soften her attitude.

The masked prosecutor regarded the Dwarf with the Horse and Pedro for a long silent moment.

"Eloquently put," she said with a cold smile. "Unfortunately Interfold law does not recognise equine testimony and so, persuasive though some may consider..." — her eyes flicked along Pedro's flank — "such testimony, you have the legal relevance of a well-hung cheval sandwich."

Pedro flinched and stepped behind the Dwarf for protection.

"And so," she continued, looking intently at the Dwarf, "I have no alternative but to find *you* guilty of being present in Interfold illegally without permit or papers and in possession of unlicensed livestock."

"But..." the Dwarf attempted to protest.

"You are fortunate that the punishment for this crime is mere expulsion and a lifelong prohibition on entering Interfold territory, wherever or whenever that is, has been or may be located." She snapped long manicured fingers and a triumvirate of ASSIIR agents reappeared. "Escort them to the south-west exit and make sure they leave by sunset, whenever that is," she instructed the eunuchs.

"Next case," the cute and yet frosty clerk called, ushering them all away with her clipboard. "Next case. Clear the chamber. Clear the chamber," she said as she waved the Dwarf with the Horse, Pedro and their escorts from the chamber.

6 In contrast the Girl with Nine Lives found her audience with the red-suited councillor a not unsatisfactory affair. On the other hand Doctor Klown considered the proposed sentence quite preposterous.

"Come, come, Councillor, you cannot seriously consider a sentence of physical mutilation an appropriate punishment," he blustered. "Even if it could be proven that my patient here is an illegal alien, which I can assure you she is not."

"I have explained my position, Doctor; I do not intend to repeat it. My decision is final and binding for having been stated aloud in the appropriate form of words laid down in Interfold law. I judge the crime committed, but in acknowledgement of your testimony I reduce the sentence. You will take the prisoner back to the hospital and perform surgery to remove her left leg at the knee."

"But..." Doctor Klown started to protest again.

"No *but,* no concession, no quarter, Doctor Klown. If you don't acknowledge your statutory duty here and now I will have you arrested on a charge of constitutional breach. Do you understand?"

"But I protest, Councillor, my patient is a long-standing Interfold resident and legally so."

"You are trying my patience, Doctor!" She glowered. "I will say this one last time. I have taken your testimony into account; the leniency of the sentence reflects this. One leg and one week of servitude, after which your patient can remain in Interfold providing after that time she has produced the appropriate legally defined documentation."

"But—"

"THIS SESSION IS OVER. Clerk: clear the court. Agents: take them both away." She turned her back on the doctor and the Girl with Nine Lives.

"Clear the chamber, clear the chamber." The cute yet frosty clerk chased them with her clipboard from the chamber and back into the custody of the triumvirate of ASSIIR agents waiting outside.

"You are to escort them back to the hospital," Frosty said to the agents, "and report back to me when the operation to remove her left leg at the knee is complete. You are to bring the limb in question to me. The councillor requires it as proof that her instructions have been carried out."

The agents nodded their acceptance of the brief and led the doctor and the Girl with Nine Lives away.

The doctor was disconsolate. "I am so sorry," he said. "There was nothing more that I could do. I shall write a letter of protest to the Council this afternoon."

"Please, Doctor," the Girl replied, quite unperturbed,

"there really is no need. I do not think things went too badly."

"Not too badly!"

"Not too badly," she continued. "The punishment could have been more severe."

"More severe?"

"Yes, more severe," she said. "You know their reputation as well as I. So all in all I am not dissatisfied with the outcome. It is only half a leg."

"Only!" Doctor Klown exclaimed. "Only half a leg!"

"Yes," she continued. "Only half a leg, and in any case..." — she paused — "it will soon grow back." She allowed the ASSIIR agents to lead her into the elevator, leaving the incredulous doctor to follow.

7 Black McCarthy was led by the Frosty Cuteness to a different chamber some distance along several dark corridors. The last of these ended with a nondescript blue door that otherwise presented a dead end.

"Go through there," the clerk ordered, "and after your audience wait here until I collect you."

"OK," Black assured her absently, giving his main focus to the unmarked, unremarkable door.

"I mean it, Mr McCarthy," she continued in stern reproach. "Do not under any circumstances go wandering off on your own. I do not want the circumstances of your uncontrollable curiosity besmirching the otherwise perfect record of my tenure. Do you understand?"

Black said nothing but nodded as he stared at the door.

"I shall return in one hour. Do not leave until I return. Wait for me if I am not present when you exit." She turned without further comment and strode away with firm, stern echoing footsteps.

Alone, Black tried the round brass door handle. He turned it to the right and pushed. Nothing. He turned it to the left and pulled. Nothing. He tried the inverse of both variations but the door seemed unwilling to open. He turned round to call the frosty yet cute clerk back to assist.

"Excuse me..." he began, but she had gone. He stared

along the gloomy and empty corridor, and wondered how long an hour would feel.

A loud clunk of the door unlocking and a creak of hinges behind him answered his question. He turned to find the door standing open a few centimetres. He pushed it wider, his hand on the round brass handle, and stepped through. The door closed behind him the moment he took his hand from the handle. Without surprise Black heard the lock connect.

He was standing in a deserted concrete courtyard. A plain grey wall formed one side of the square immediately opposite the door by which he had entered. This otherwise unremarkable façade held two huge blue doors, some ten metres high. The other sides of the courtyard were composed of unbroken stone and so the doors formed the only other means of access to or exit from the courtyard.

Black took the fact that one door stood ajar as his next instruction. He strode across the small square, paused for a moment and then entered.

His eyes were barely adjusted to the expansive dark interior when two huge bronze lions, three or four times the size of their brethren in Trafalgar Square, leapt into life before him. Tossing their heads and roaring at a formidable barrage of decibels, they pawed the ground not a metre from him with their huge metal feet, while thrashing the ground with long and impressive tails thicker than the thigh of a man.

At the same time two gigantic metal cedars seemed to spring fully formed from the ground to his left and to his right. The branches of each tree lined with glittering silver martins and golden swifts, each exquisitely crafted and all twittering in song. This rose to a crescendo as the lions receded a few paces to regard him with ill-concealed suspicion.

Many metres above him, Black became conscious of a huge stone throne with smoke billowing around it. One moment it was high above his head in the distant eves, the next right before him at ground level. At this the lions leapt forward once more and the birdsong exploded again. Smoke billowed, obscuring all, and out of the smoke a figure walked towards him.

She was in her early fifties, little more than five feet tall. Stocky, dressed in a tweed suit of skirt and jacket, she approached Black with one arm folded across her body holding the elbow of the other, which held aloft a fat cigar. She stopped a metre from him and raised a hand, at which signal all noise ceased. She stared into his eyes and smoke curled like a moustache from both nostrils.

"I," she said, "am the Dragon Lady."

"Hello," Black said, offering a hand. "My name is—"

"I know full well who you are, boy, and why you are here." She waved his hand aside. "Who do you think summoned you? It is only at my bidding that you are here now and only because I permit it that you are present in Interfold at all."

"I see," Black said, not seeing at all.

"Do you?" she shot back. "Do you, McCarthy? Ha! I suspect you do not. Let me tell you a thing or two, McCarthy, some of which you may understand, some of which you may not. The city of Constantine was immune to neither Saracen nor Crusader in the end, and so shall it be for Interfold if you do not uncover the stone beneath which the man you seek is hiding."

The Dragon Lady exhaled and smoke curled again from her nostrils, even though the smouldering cigar was pinched between the forefinger and thumb of her right hand and used to gesture as she spoke.

"Forgive me if you find me a sphinx, McCarthy, but you have no idea what it is your masters have you embarked upon. They send you to me a lamb. Do they dare me to send you back a wolf?"

Startled and uncomprehending but conscious that here before him was someone of great power and influence in Interfold, Black shuddered but fought to keep his bewilderment hidden.

"Do you mean to say that you can help me in my hunt for Eugenides?" he asked.

"No," the Dragon Lady replied.

"No," Black said.

"No."

"But why ever not, if you need him found?"

"Because if I knew where to find him I would have no use for you, and would not have permitted your presence in Interfold. Really, boy! Are you always this slow? It is a wonder you ever solve a case!"

"Then why am I here?" Black asked.

"Because, dear lad, the condition under which I will allow you to remain in Interfold is that henceforth you will work first and foremost for me and for Interfold. You are hereby turned, McCarthy. There is no choice for you in this matter.

Welcome to the dark night of the double agent." She raised her cigar in a toast to the shadows.

"And what if I refuse?" Black asked.

"Refuse?"

"Yes, refuse."

"Well, I don't know," she mused, "not having ever encountered anyone foolish enough to refuse my request. I am unused to such a turn of events. Let me think, McCarthy." She paused, tapped her temple with her finger before stepping closer to him. She looked him square in the eyes and said with quiet authority, "You do not want to know what evil consequences will befall you if you are fool enough to refuse to do my bidding, McCarthy. Do you understand?"

"Yes," Black replied, although he was far from sure that he did, "I understand."

"Good." She smiled a grim smile. "You find this, this Mordechai you call Eugenides and you bring him to me. I must have my Greek fire, McCarthy, and you are the one who is going to bring it to me. Dixon here will provide you with arms." She gestured to a grim, bald Bristolian who had emerged from the shadows. "You are hereby authorised to carry arms in Interfold and to use them in reasonable execution of any who seek to hinder your mission. And when I say reasonable execution, McCarthy, I mean reasonable execution. I do not want Interfold alarmed by bloodshed, do you understand?"

"Yes," Black assured her, "I understand."

"And, McCarthy..."

"Yes, ma'am?"

"Please make some efforts to be discreet." The Dragon Lady turned and walked away into the dark interior of the building, leaving Black in the hands of Dixon.

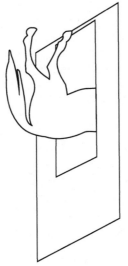

CHAPTER EIGHT

The Man Who Dreamt He Was Dreaming was dreaming he was dreaming. He had kicked down into a deep layer of sleep in his search for a degree of gratification or relief.

The dream of the girl in the wet pink panties was long gone. Neither she nor the thin red girl had reappeared in any of the fragments of dreams through which he had segued since the girl with the long wet hair had last stabbed him.

He had stumbled in and out of scenes he did not recognise as emanating from his life. Echoes of real events they may have been, but from when he could not recall.

He found himself in a crowd and could see a fair distance away in the throng the gigantic form of the Man Who Lived in a Vacuum Cleaner in furtive and earnest conversation with someone the Man Who Dreamt He Was Dreaming could not see clearly. The Man Who Dreamt He Was Dreaming tried to get the attention of the Man Who Lived in a Vacuum Cleaner, but without success. There was something about the silhouette of the other party and something disturbing about the countenance of the Man Who Lived in a Vacuum Cleaner that concerned the Man Who Dreamt He Was Dreaming.

He tried to push forward, but the tide of the crowd was flowing against him and forbade any progress. The Man Who Lived in a Vacuum Cleaner receded from his correspondent with a gesture of intense frustration. He pushed through the crowd away from the Man Who Dreamt He Was Dreaming and the other frustratingly familiar figure and merged into the ill-formed features of the crowd.

The Man Who Dreamt He Was Dreaming stopped still and allowed the bodies to swirl around him. Watched as the Man Who Lived in a Vacuum Cleaner became but a shadow. A hand slipped under his arm as he frowned with concern for his former customer. He turned to look at the brunette by his side with a bob and black wire-rimmed glasses.

"You might as well come up for some coffee," she said, "now that he has gone."

The Man Who Dreamt He Was Dreaming considered his options. On the one hand he was trying hard to recall whether this was an important recollection of something that he should remember, but, on the other, this was a dream and the brunette was as cute as he found himself thirsty. Coffee did sound good, but this was of course just the sort of invitation that usually led to trouble. All things considered, though, he was as ever inclined to drift with the current of the dream, follow the girl and see what transpired.

"Coffee," he said, "would be good."

The brunette with the bob led him through the crowd, through a doorway, up some stairs and into her apartment. He sat in the centre of a cream leather sofa while the girl went to make coffee.

Nothing changed for what seemed many minutes. No sound came from the kitchen to imply the creation of coffee. He waited and he waited. He thought again of the troubled countenance of the Man Who Lived in a Vacuum Cleaner and immediately he was back outside in the midst of the crowd, watching a repeat performance of the departure of the Man Who Lived in a Vacuum Cleaner. He shook his head, concerned again that this had some significance that he was unable to fathom and unable to recall from his sleep-battered memory.

She led him away much as before but this time took the precaution of not leaving the room.

"So much for the coffee," he said.

"Sorry?"

"I said so much for the coffee."

"Coffee?"

"Yes, coffee," he said.

"What coffee?" she asked, mystified.

"It doesn't matter," he assured her, hoping that this was true.

"OK," she said, "no problem."

He sat again in the centre of the cream leather sofa and watched, indifferent, as she unbuttoned her blouse and let it fall at his feet. He fought the thought of the Man Who Lived in a Vacuum Cleaner as she unzipped her skirt. Failed and turned his head towards the window.

Immediately he was back out in the crowd, watching and calling as the Man Who Lived in a Vacuum Cleaner made his final emphatic negative gesture, turned and strode away.

She was less patient this time, tugging at his arm to hurry him on their way. In a moment he was once more seated on the cream leather sofa watching the brunette with the bob disrobe. Skirt followed blouse to the floor. He stared at the discarded articles as black bra, black panties and her brunette bob were added to the heap.

Alarmed too late, he failed to comprehend the all-too-usual danger. She sank every inch of the long-bladed knife into his chest with slow precision. Heel kicked him in the head with such force that he felt his real slumbering self jolt where he lay.

A second later it was over. A second later all was spinning black velocity. A second later he went crashing down down down en route to another dream of a dream of a dream.

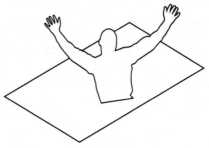

CHAPTER NINE

1 Black McCarthy returned to the Red Light Basement confused, bewildered and armed to the teeth. Dixon had supplied him with a discreet arsenal of weaponry all of which was designed to dispatch a foe with maximum precision and minimum fuss, even in the hands of an untrained marksman like Black.

Finding himself dually employed, and with the added complication of Joylin's bloodlust, his first instinct was to run like hell to a safe location. The current position of INTERFOLD — The Time Travel ~~Hotel~~ Republic ruled this out. This much was clear even to Black. As an alternative he therefore sought the safety of familiar comforts within his, for the time being at least, favourite bar.

"You look like a man who could use some coffee," Moe said, or will say or may well be saying at this very moment.

"Strong and black," Black said, positioning himself at the bar. "It has already been one hell of a morning."

"One Red Light Espresso coming up," Moe said.

Black sat in silent contemplation of the empty bar as Moe busied himself with a complex-looking contraption that was in fact the patented INTERFOLD Italian Espresso Majestic no. 6, a huge and formidable piece of catering engineering that, although capable of delivering some very fine coffee indeed, was only available in pink.

After much complicated manipulation of the INTERFOLD Italian Espresso Majestic no. 6 and an astonishing quantity of steam, a red-faced Moe placed a small white porcelain cup of the Red Light Basement's finest espresso in front of Black McCarthy and stood back to mop his brow with a paper towel.

"That is the best cup of coffee you will drink in Interfold," he said. "No one else's brew comes close."

"I am sure it is, Moe," Black said, regarding the steaming cup. "Can you get me a glass with this much ice?" He indicated about an inch and a half with forefinger and thumb.

"Sure," Moe said, curious but obliging. He scooped some ice into a glass and set it on a paper coaster beside Black's as yet untouched Red Light Espresso. "There you go."

"Thanks," Black said, and he immediately tipped the hot espresso over the ice.

"What the hell?" Moe leapt in alarm, throwing his hands up to his face. "What are you doing to that fine espresso, McCarthy? Did you not hear me say it was the best in all Interfold?"

"The best in all Interfold?" Black asked.

"Yes. The best in all Interfold."

"Then it will be the best iced espresso in all Interfold like this." He lifted the glass in a toast to his host and tipped it down his throat in one easy action. "Great snakes!" he exclaimed. Followed by "Caramba!"

"I told you," Moe said with a smile of smug satisfaction tempered only by his remaining horror at the whole ice scenario. He turned away to serve the Girl with the Broken Neck, who had dropped in for a take-out on her way to work.

Left alone with his thoughts again and with strong coffee on board, Black contemplated his predicament with caffeine-fuelled clarity. Decisive action was called for. What form this action should take he knew not, but the need for action was clear.

Joylin, of course, was to be avoided. She could prove

useful but the price looked on the high side. Double agent he may now be, but the Wolf paid well for Black's services and that in Black's book gave him priority. If the Wolf wanted Eugenides found then Black would find him. If he subsequently informed the Dragon Lady of his whereabouts, where was the harm? As long as the necessary funds from the Wolf were fully cleared in Black's account before he did so and a swift exit from INTERFOLD had been arranged, Black saw no problem.

Joylin was not his only information opportunity. There was also the Nurse with the Curse and the new possibilities that the Girl with Nine Lives presented. The Man Who Fell Through Floors was a useful fellow who not only knew his way around INTERFOLD but also appeared to have mastered the knack of gaining access beyond locked doors.

The Girl with Nine Lives had last been seen entering a courtroom and Floors was currently unaccounted for; the Nurse with the Curse he would see later. How useful any of them would be he could assess in due course, and whichever he met first he would enlist first in the hope that this would at a minimum help to determine the next step.

A plan established, he looked up to order another glass of Moe's fine iced espresso.

"And then," he heard the Girl with the Broken Neck say to Moe, "she ate my food, borrowed my clothes and hurried off into Interfold muttering about how some guy might think he had successfully disappeared but she knew where he was and he really had it coming."

"What?" Black asked. "Did you say someone who had disappeared?"

"I think that is what she said," she replied.

"Are you sure?"

"To the best of my recollection," the Girl with the Broken Neck replied.

"Did she mention his name?" Black asked.

"His name?"

"Yes, his name," Black confirmed.

"I don't think so," the Girl with the Broken Neck said, "but now you mention it I am not all that sure. I was cooking some eggs at the time."

"So she is looking for someone who does not want to be found?"

"Yes."

"And who was this girl?" Black asked, flipping into interrogation mode.

"As I was saying to Moe," the Girl with the Broken Neck explained, "I have no idea. It was the strangest thing. She crept up on me, kicked me in the neck and broke into my apartment. I hadn't even eaten breakfast! Claimed she was an assassin."

"An assassin?" Black asked.

"Yes, an assassin. Quite mad, most likely."

"Let's hope so."

"Must dash, Moe. Thanks for the coffee." She waved at Moe. "Good to meet you, Mr...?"

"McCarthy," Black said, unconsciously tilting his neck to match the uncomfortable angle at which the girl was wearing her head. "Black McCarthy."

"You look worried, old boy," Moe said, removing the empty glass and cup from the bar. "Another?"

"What?" Black asked, distracted. "Oh, yes, another would be good, Moe. Thanks."

"My name is Dave," Moe said as he turned to the patented INTERFOLD Italian Espresso Majestic no. 6.

"Of course it is," Black said to himself, and he turned to stare across the bar. The Girl with the Broken Neck could have been mistaken, but it was too much of a coincidence. It looked like Black would have to contend with the unwelcome competition of a rival in his search for Eugenides.

2 Upstairs, Alex from Mars was struggling. The third attempt at her inflationary experiment had made little perceivable difference and, although she had thrown herself into example four with dogged persistence and enthusiasm, it had not gone well.

"I am sorry," she told the Man Who Lived in a Vacuum Cleaner as she stopped mid-application, "but this is making my neck ache. We will have to try a different approach."

"A different approach?" he asked, looking around, wondering what, given his minute stature, she could mean.

"Yes, a different approach," she repeated. "What if I lie here with my head on the pillow and turn to face you? You can do the work, so to speak, while I rest my neck. Shall we try that?"

"OK," the little man agreed, "let's give it a try. I don't want you to be uncomfortable."

And so, with one hand resting on her nose and the other on her chin, the Man Who Lived in a Vacuum Cleaner slipped the surprisingly large penis into the scientific mouth of Alex from Mars and began to gently thrust between her puckered lips.

"Everything OK?" he enquired.

"Mmm mmm," Alex replied, winking at him in encouragement.

"Here we go then," he said, picking up speed and feeling for some reason that he was duty-bound to provide a commentary. "Yes sir-ee. Oh yes indeed."

On and on he went, jabbering away inanely. Alex closed her eyes and thought of Mars, zoning out farther than she had intended, and failed to take note of the warning in the rising tone of the Man Who Lived in a Vacuum Cleaner's voice.

"Ho. Ho. HO HO HO..." he exclaimed as he approached the peak. "HO oh oh HO HO HO," like some demented Santa Claus delivering an unwholesome gift. A wave of dizziness overcame him at this critical juncture. He lost his grip on nose and chin. His head spun and eyes and ears filled with white noise. He stumbled backwards, thrust forwards and jabbed the surprisingly large penis straight up Alex's right nostril.

"OW!" Alex said, zoning right back in just in time for the Man Who Lived in a Vacuum Cleaner to pull back and shoot a voluminous (given his stature) jet of goo straight in her eye.

The Man Who Lived in a Vacuum Cleaner fell back on the bed, overwhelmed by the sensation of the room spinning around him. Alex from Mars, however, was indignant.

"Bloody hell!" she said. Holding a hand to her burning eye, she ran for the bathroom.

The Man Who Lived in a Vacuum Cleaner was feeling pleased and impressed not only with the generous helping he had produced but that he had remained conscious for the first time in four attempts. So much so that he had entirely failed to notice that Alex was absent.

She returned a few minutes later wrapped in an INTERFOLD bathrobe that, like so much in INTERFOLD, was only available in one size (at least two sizes too small) and one colour: pink. She stood over the Man Who Lived in a Vacuum Cleaner and fumed.

"I don't care what Earth etiquette is about these things," she told him, "but where I come from that sort of thing is most definitely on the list of things for which you *ask permission first!*"

"I'm sorry," the bemused Man Who Lived in a Vacuum Cleaner said, not knowing where he had transgressed. "What do you mean?"

"You know EXACTLY what I mean!" she said. "You know what you just did."

"Do I?" he asked.

"Of course you do."

"Of course I do," he agreed, feeling this was probably the safest way to proceed for the time being. They had a long way to go, after all.

"HA!" Alex exclaimed and she stomped back into the bathroom, shutting the door between them with a firm heel.

3 The Dwarf with the Horse would have been migrating north once more were it not for his and Pedro's ongoing entanglement with the INTERFOLD law enforcement system. They remained in the custody of the original triumvirate of ASSIIR agents who had escorted them to their hearing and who were now charged with executing their expulsion from INTERFOLD — The Time Travel ~~Hotel~~ Republic. This was not proving straightforward as a typically INTERFOLDian elevator shortage was once again a complicating factor. The ASSIIR agents were arguing about the fastest route to the south-west exit. The Dwarf with the Horse was inclined to leave them to it and wait patiently for an opportunity for escape.

"I am not taking that horse down the staircase," said the agent who had most closely experienced the effect that stairway terror had on Pedro. He was still wearing an olfactory reminder of the previous incident and was in no hurry to repeat it.

"We are not asking you to," the first of his colleagues said.

"We need to find an elevator," the second added.

"An elevator?"

"Yes. An elevator," No. 2 confirmed.

"An elevator," No. 1 cut in, "that connects with the western basement."

"Or at least," No. 2 said, "that connects with a level that connects with that level."

"Or connects with a level that does," No. 1 added for clarification.

"Just as long as you are clear," No. 3 said, "I am not taking that horse down any stairwell. Not now, not ever. For all I care they can wander around this level for all Interfold time."

"Whatever that means," No. 2 added with a smile.

"Yeah, whatever that means," No. 1 agreed.

"Are you laughing at me?" No. 3 asked, staring at his fellows. "I am an Agent for State Security and Intelligence of the Interfold Republic and I demand a little more respect from my fellow agents." He pointed a petulant finger at them to indicate that he was serious.

"Calm down," No. 1 assured him. "We are on your side."

"Yeah, calm down," No. 2 added. "We want to find an elevator as much as you do."

"Of course we do," No. 1 agreed, "but you know as well as we do that vertical transportation capacity is a scarce resource throughout the Interfold Republic."

"Not to mention this level," No. 2 said.

"Absolutely," No. 1 added.

"And not only are they on the rare side..."

"They are frequently rather small."

"Precisely," No. 2 said.

"Exactly," said No. 1.

ASSIIR Agent No. 3 just glowered at them and said nothing more and continued to follow the Dwarf and Pedro, who were now leading the way. His colleagues looked at each other and shrugged.

4 Black McCarthy sat with his hands resting backs-down on the bar in the Red Light Basement and his face buried in his hands.

"Bugger. Bugger. Bugger. Bugger," he said quietly over and over again. "Bugger. Bugger. Bugger."

"Hey, buddy. What's the problem?" the Man Who Fell

or Falls, Is Falling, Has Fallen or Will Fall Through Floors asked, falling through the ceiling, conducting a somersault mid-air and landing on a stool beside Black.

Black looked up. Stared at the Man Who Fell Through Floors for a moment before straightening up.

"It's just a work thing," he said.

"Yeah?" Floors asked. "You sure I can't help?"

"I don't know."

"You don't know?"

"No," Black said, "I don't know."

"Maybe Moe and I can help somehow," Floors said. Moe nodded. "You look like you could at least use sharing the problem."

Black hesitated. "Well, I am meant to work alone. It's kind of a rule of the trade. Not to mention contractual obligation."

"But who is going to know?"

"Yeah," Moe said, "I am not about to tell anyone."

"Nor me," said the Man Who Fell Through Floors.

"That's really kind of you guys, but..." Black began.

"What have you got to lose?" the Man Who Fell Through Floors asked.

"Give us a try," Moe added, polishing a glass with a grubby tea towel.

"I don't know," Black said again. "I don't know."

Moe looked at the Man Who Fell Through Floors and at Black in turn, a thought running through his mind.

"Alack!" he said loudly. "Behold the fearful porpentine!"

"The what?" the Man Who Fell Through Floors asked, half amused, half appalled. Black just stared at Moe, incredulous.

"It's from Shakespeare," Dave said.

"Are you sure?" asked the Man Who Fell Through Floors.

"I think so."

"Which play?"

"*Macbeth*, I think, or *King Lear*."

"*Macbeth*?" Black asked.

"Yes," Moe said, "or *King Lear*. I forget which."

"It wasn't *The Tempest*?" the Man Who Fell Through Floors asked.

"Or *Hamlet*?" asked Black.

"No," Moe said. "It is definitely *Macbeth* or *King Lear*. But you miss my point."

"Your point?" Black asked.

"Yes, my point," Dave said.

"Which is?" the Man Who Fell Through Floors asked.

"Well, less a point than..."

"Than what?"

"A metaphor."

"A metaphor?" Black asked.

"Yes, a metaphor," Moe said.

"For what?"

"A thorny problem."

"A thorny problem?" the Man Who Fell Through Floors asked.

"Yes," Moe said. "I thought it might help to have a distraction. You know, to bring a fresh perspective to whatever ails our friend."

The Man Who Fell Through Floors stared at Moe with a smile spreading slowly across his mouth.

"What an excellent idea, Moe," he said. "I am very impressed."

"Thank you."

"Incidentally," the Man Who Fell Through Floors said, "did you know that men who masturbate regularly have a significantly reduced chance of developing prostate cancer?"

"I didn't know that," Moe said.

"Is that relevant?" Black asked.

"How often is regularly?"

"More than five times per week."

"Five times per week?"

"No. More than five. Six as a minimum to qualify."

"Qualify? You make it sound like you get frequent flyer points."

"Be a bonus if you did."

"Sure thing. Beat cancer and get a free flight!"

"Interesting though this is," Black said, "how is this relevant?"

"It is not literally relevant," Floors admitted, "but I think Moe here is right. An excursion might be just the thing to help."

"An excursion?"

"Yes. An excursion."

"What? Masturbate your way to Madagascar?" Black asked, thinking that would take a heap of frequent flyer points and much hard, if diverting, work.

"No, no. Not literally," the Man Who Fell Through Floors

said. "It is a creative technique."

"A creative technique."

"Yes, a creative technique," the Man Who Fell Through Floors said, "to help generate ideas."

"Ideas?" Black asked.

"Yes, ideas. The idea is that you distract yourself to free your mind to conjure up a fresh angle on whatever problem is distracting you from finding the solution to the problem at hand. It is called an excursion."

"Like a fishing trip," Dave said.

"Exactly!" the Man Who Fell Through Floors exclaimed. "Thank you, Moe. A fishing trip is the perfect idea. Why didn't we think of it before?"

"No idea," Black said, wondering how a fishing trip was relevant. "I didn't think an actual excursion like a fishing trip was the point."

"You misunderstand, Black; the fishing trip is the idea, not the excursion," the Man Who Fell Through Floors said.

Black looked blankly at Floors and Moe. "Of course!" he said, not understanding at all but hoping he would get away with it. "So we are going fishing?"

"Yes, we are," the Man Who Fell Through Floors said. "Are you up for it, Moe?"

"Never miss an opportunity to fish," Dave said.

"So where are we going?" Black asked. He had no idea whether downtown Phnom Penh was famous for its fishing, his meagre geographical knowledge not including any information on the fishing potential of the Mekong.

"Underground," the Man Who Fell Through Floors said.

"Underground?"

"Yes. Underground."

5   While Black was failing to understand the reasoning behind an underground fishing trip, the good doctor was flailing around up in the ER in what he felt was a perfectly reasonable attempt at delay.

"Anything, Nurse?" he demanded of the Nurse with the Curse. "Anything at all we can use as an excuse for a delay? Blood pressure? Allergies? Absence of adequate medical supplies? An unclean operating environment? There must be something."

"Please try and keep calm, Doctor," the Nurse urged him.

"Her blood pressure is normal. She has no allergies. We have more medical supplies than we will ever have use for, and our operating environment is exceptionally clean and very much the *finest in the district*." She smiled.

"What?" Doctor Klown asked, not understanding.

"*The finest in the district*," the Nurse said quoted again, trying not to giggle, "*completely uncontaminated* in any way."

"Are you sure?"

"Absolutely. It has never been used and we sterilised it just this morning. It is the cleanest of the clean. It will make a refreshing change to have reason to put it to use."

"I suppose you are right in that respect," the doctor conceded, "but it is still a ludicrous and barbaric response to a trifling incident in my book, Nurse."

"Are you two going to stay in here arguing all day or is one of you going to come and bite my leg off?" the Girl with Nine Lives asked, standing in the doorway of Doctor Klown's office with her hands on her hips. She was wearing one of those terrible hospital gowns that gapes at the back. She had put it on back to front and was thus flashing her stripes at the poor doctor, who found himself desperate not to look but compelled to all the same.

"Bite... leg... whatever d-d-do you mean?" he stammered.

"How else do you plan to remove it?" the Girl with Nine Lives asked.

"Well..." the doctor began, looking to the Nurse for support, "ordinarily we would use a surgical device designed for such a purpose."

"A surgical device for biting off legs?"

"Not for biting, exactly..." the Nurse said.

"How else can it be done?"

The Nurse with the Curse looked at Doctor Klown. Doctor Klown looked at the Nurse.

"Our state-of-the-art surgical instrument is" — Doctor Klown paused — "not for biting, so to speak, more for... sawing."

"Sawing?" the Girl with Nine Lives asked, appalled.

"Yes, sawing," the doctor said.

"You people are barbaric," the Girl said in disgust.

"I assure you it is quite normal."

"Ridiculous. You call yourselves a civilised society and yet you go about sawing people's legs off when a good clean bite would do the job in a jiffy with a fraction of the fuss.

You will tell me next that you don't even have a hospital dog!"

Doctor Klown and the Nurse with the Curse exchanged a worried look. Concern for the sanity of their patient communicated between them.

"No," the Nurse began, taking the Girl with Nine Lives gently by the arm, "we don't have a hospital dog, but we do have the finest operating theatre in the district."

"Theatre?" the Girl with Nine Lives echoed, her blood rising. "Theatre? I am not putting on a bloody performance. There was no mention of a public mutilation. All I need you people to do is bite my bloody leg off so that I can get out of the hospital and on with the rest of the sentence. Is that too much to ask?"

"Not that kind of theatre," the Nurse said in a gentle and, she hoped, soothing voice. "It is just what it is called in England."

"England?" the Girl with Nine Lives asked. "England? But we are not in England; we are in Interfold, and in my experience that means you should take nothing for granted."

"Please try not to worry," Doctor Klown said, ushering the Nurse with the Curse and the Girl with Nine Lives in the general direction of the operating theatre/room. "I am an accomplished surgeon and this is a very straightforward procedure, although the recovery time can of course stretch into months."

The Girl with Nine Lives stopped in surprise and looked squarely at the doctor.

"What do you mean by months?" she asked.

"Now, now, I don't mean to worry you but we have to be realistic about this. Loss of a limb is something that one doesn't just bounce back from. It will take time for you to adjust. Post-operative pain management will be our priority and once the wound starts to heal we can look at your options. We have to be sensible about the time frame, however, and we are talking months, not weeks."

"Enough fooling around now, Doctor!" The Girl with Nine Lives laughed. "You very nearly had me with that whole sawing thing, but you blew it with all that 'months and months of recovery' nonsense. Come on, Doctor and Nurse, enough is enough."

"Whatever do you mean?" Doctor Klown asked, confused anew.

"You both know as well as I do that it will take hardly any time at all. My leg will have grown back within a fortnight."

"A fortnight?" a stunned Nurse with the Curse said.

"Yes, a fortnight," the Girl with Nine Lives said. "Now where is that dog?"

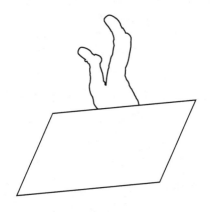

CHAPTER TEN

The Man Who Dreamt He Was Dreaming was dreaming he was waking up. From dream after dream and sleep after sleep. Bang. He was up. He was awake / he was asleep. He was on the move. Ascendent. Like a diver from the deep. Bends-ridden and bewildered by the cacophony of mini-dream and micro-mare. Bang. He was up. With disembodied hands about his arm. With a knife in his guts and a hook in his chest. With the scratch of the hangman's hemp about his neck. Bang. He was up. He was up. He was dreaming he was dreaming he was moving relentlessly back up through layer after layer of imprisonment and spell. Through week after week in the hole. In the cell. Bang. He was up and he was running.

He was running. They were after him and if they caught him he was going to get a kicking. He pulled his hood further up. His cap peak down. Pushed the bandana back over his nose. Over-shoulder look to check. Still there. Gaining. Are they gaining?

Back where he had run from, the flames splashed orange off the night sky. Stars scattered underfoot in a billion grains of shattered glass. Sirens, screams and alarms. Shouts, cries of pain, curses and yells. The crash of truncheon on shield, on body, on bone. Blood and snot shining on the steel-toe-capped boots of the police. Protestors fighting on but falling back. Flags flying black and red. Cars burning. Buildings burning. Smoke and pepper spray washed down with water cannon.

A *zzzzooommmm* and a *zzzzzip* and a rubber bullet whizzed past. He heard it a second after he felt the cold whoosh of air on his cheek.

"THIS WAY," a woman shouted to him. "THIS WAY." He looked across at her. She was standing calm on a street corner like a steward directing a fun run. "Head for the power station. We will regroup there."

He stopped and stared at her. She looked oddly familiar but he couldn't say why. He had the weird feeling that she knew him and he knew her, but in that moment he could not say how.

"KEEP GOING," she shouted at him. "COME ON." She started running and he followed. Hundreds of others up ahead doing the same.

It was exactly as he would recall if you asked him. The moment when he realised that the protest had morphed from an ugly fight with the police into a riot choreographed by female stewards in high-vis vests. Acting like a funnel they directed the fleeing crowd across Chelsea Bridge. Stoked the mood of the protest so that anger rose as they ran. There was something in the air, and it wasn't just the tear gas. A whiff of revolution. The scent of something planned.

Before he knew it he was in the thick of a fast-moving crowd filing through a gate in the tall hoarding and barbed-wire wall that encircled the site on which the ruins of Battersea Power Station stood. Platforms had been thrown up against the inside of this hoarding-wall and people were climbing up. Others were passing up bricks, rocks and rubble. Bottles with rags poking out of their necks and other ammunition.

The Man Who Dreamt He Was Dreaming stood as faceless fellow protesters whirled around him. Turning in a slow circle, growing wary. Through the crowd a woman was walking towards him. She was tall and slim with dark brown hair tied back for practicality. It was the Girl with Nine Lives.

Younger, less worn down, quite beautiful.

"Welcome to the occupation," she said. She wore a yellow high-vis jacket and carried an old-fashioned walkie-talkie which looked like it had been stolen from a museum of communication devices. He stared at her.

"You!" he said, suspicious and guilty.

"WHAT?" she shouted back over the cacophony of voices suddenly all shouting at once.

He turned round just in time to see the gates through which he had come slam closed. Just in time to catch a glimpse of the advancing wall of riot shields behind which the police were taking mobile refuge as the bricks and rocks began to rain on them.

"Get up on the barricades," the Girl with Nine Lives shouted at him. It was an order, not a request. "Or else hand up some ammo."

With a growing sense of unease he did as he recalled he had done. Memory and dream working in startling synchronicity. He climbed up onto a platform and crouched on a scaffold plank, catching his breath, before standing up and hurling a brick over the top in the general direction of the police.

He ducked back down as the plastic bullets thumped into the hoarding wall and tear gas canisters flew up and over to drop down far inside the perimeter. Another brick was thrust into his hand from below. He counted to three. Levered himself up. Left hand gripping a scaffold pole. Right arm extended, ready to bowl the brick. But as he prepared to throw everything went all science fiction on him. A brilliant clinical white light filled the world behind him and a weird unearthly high-pitched whine suffocated all other sound. His arm dropped and he stood up straight and turned back to look towards the source of the light and sound. Towards the power station which was flickering in and out of existence. There and then gone. Gone and then there. Everyone was standing staring. The police beyond the wall forgotten by everyone except the female stewards in the high-vis vests. They were all talking furtively into their antique communication devices.

It was the moment when he knew a gutted and ruined power station and the large area of the site around it flipped away to be replaced by INTERFOLD — The Time Travel ~~Hotel~~ Republic, which had chosen, is choosing or will choose at some point yet to be determined that exact moment to arrive from some future incarnation of Battersea Power Station and put an end to all further debate about that iconic London landmark.

He stood shielding his eyes and then, for some stupid reason that he knew was a mistake even as he made it, he turned round and looked back over the barricade in the direction of the police. A female police officer was standing clear of the riot shields, unclipping her helmet and visor. She dropped them at her side as she loosened her long dark hair like she was auditioning for a shampoo ad. She dropped to one knee, raised her gun and fired with a knowing smile, twisting her mouth. She made eye contact at the exact moment that the rubber bullet hit him squarely in the chest and kicked him up and off the scaffold plank.

He fell and everything went out.

He fell and there was nothing else.

He fell down and down and down.

There was no ground and he kept on falling.

And falling.

And falling.

And falling.

Until he finally hit the ground and woke up like he had been kicked in the face. Sucking in desperate breath. Fingers massaging the place where the dream bullet had hit him in the chest. He woke up. And this time... he was awake.

CHAPTER ELEVEN

1 Black McCarthy was underground, or further underground given that he had started out in the Red Light Basement, which, as its name rather gives away, is of course below the ground floor (following as it does the British model of floor designation) of the south-western corner of the complex micro-conurbation that is **INTERFOLD** — The Time Travel ~~Hotel~~ Republic. He was accompanied by the Man Who Fell Through Floors and the Red Light Basement's head barman-cum-manager known as Moe, although as is well documented he insisted (quite erroneously) that his name was in fact "Dave".

Moe was leading the way down a dark spiral staircase that he had revealed by lifting a trap door in the floor behind the bar of the Red Light Basement. It seemed to Black to be similar to the spiral staircases found in dozens of ruined castles all over England. It may have been that it was more similar to the spiral staircases of castles in other countries, but as his experience of non-Anglo-Norman castle architecture was limited he could not be sure.

"Forgive me for asking," he said, "but where are we going?"

"We told you," the Man Who Fell Through Floors said. "Fishing."

"Fishing?" Black asked.

"Yes. Fishing."

"So why are we going down a staircase that quite clearly is taking us further underground? Surely we are not going fishing in a cave?"

"No. Not a cave," Dave said. "More of an underground lake."

"Or to be precise," the Man Who Fell Through Floors said, "a cistern."

"A cistern?" Black asked.

"Yes. A cistern."

"It is a sort of reservoir beneath Interfold or, more precisely, beneath the land beneath the land that Interfold has stolen on its travels," Moe said.

"I am not sure I understand what you mean," Black said with uncharacteristic honesty.

"What you have to remember," the Man Who Fell Through Floors said, "is that the area of land that Interfold originally occupied was limited to the greater site of Battersea Power Station. As the population grew with early relocations just about every square metre of that land was built upon, in places up to a great height, as I'm sure you've noticed."

"So it continued underground. Which is where the Red Light Basement came into being," Moe added.

"That's right," the Man Who Fell Through Floors said, "and then it was discovered that unbeknown to most of its inhabitants, Interfold had been quietly annexing further underground during its apparently random stays in different locations and times."

"You say 'apparently random' as if there is some doubt," Black said.

"And I mean it. While the Interfold authorities would never admit it, there are those of us who suspect a deliberate hand in the would-be erratic wanderings of the Republic."

"Too right," Moe said. "Keep up, lads. We are nearly at the quay."

"The quay?" Black asked.

"Yes. The quay."

"Fair enough. So that is where the cistern came from?"

"Exactly," the Man Who Fell Through Floors said.

"As far as we can tell, anyway," Moe said. "I arrived at the bar one morning and discovered the trap door that we came through this morning. Interfold was in Istanbul at the time."

"Constantinople," the Man Who Fell Through Floors cut in.

"What?"

"Constantinople. At the time when Interfold visited, it would still have been conventional to refer to the city as Constantinople rather than Istanbul."

"But in the contemporary timeline of Interfold Istanbul would be more accurate and in any case that is what the inhabitants of that city would call it, so why hark back to a name the city has arguably not worn since 1453? You might as well call it Byzantium."

"Don't be silly. That is well outside the time-travelling bandwidth of the Republic, as you well know."

"What?" Black asked.

"Interfold only travels within a fairly narrow time band," Moe said.

"It is one of the things that fuels our suspicion," the Man Who Fell Through Floors added.

"So what happened after you found the trap door?" Black asked in an attempt to get the conversation back on topic.

"A chap came up through it with a rod and two fine-looking fish, said *Good morning* and headed off through the bar," Moe said. "Here we are. The quay."

"Shouldn't have any trouble getting a boat," the Man Who Fell Through Floors said. "Not on a... what day is it, anyway?"

"Or was it," Moe said.

"I have no idea either way," Black said.

They had reached the bottom of the spiral staircase, which like several others snaked its way down to a long underground quay at the edge of the subterranean lake-cum-cistern. Dave and the Man Who Fell Through Floors led the way down some stone steps to the water's edge and engaged one of the many boatmen in negotiations.

"This chap will take us," Moe called back to Black, who was staring around from the people selling exotic foods and fresh fish from baskets on the quay to a steady stream of people emerging and returning through the doorways along the wall on the land side of the quay. "He says his name is Charon, but I am sure that is just a joke." He grinned at Black, on whom the joke was entirely lost.

They stepped into the boat followed by Charon, who stood at the bow and propelled them out into the cistern with the help of a long pole, gondolier-style, steering them between rows of vast pillars that disappeared into the darkness in all directions. The ceiling of the cistern was just visible arching between the tops of the pillars, the black water illuminated only by flickering flame torches in brackets on every pillar and by the oil lamps lashed to the front of every boat they passed. It was like sailing through an ordered forest of pillars in a vast extrapolation of a deeply flooded cathedral or basilica.

Black, Dave and the Man Who Fell Through Floors were silent for a while as Charon navigated, but as they cut through the water a thought occurred to Black.

"Chaps," he said, "correct me if I am wrong, but don't we need some rods or some other form of fishing equipment, or are we going to catch them with our hands?"

Moe and the Man Who Fell Through Floors looked at one another.

"We are not going fishing," Moe said.

"What?" exclaimed Black. "But you both stated several times that we were going fishing."

"We know," the Man Who Fell Through Floors said.

"It was a deliberate deception," Moe added.

"So where the hell are we going?" Black asked.

Moe looked at the Man Who Fell Through Floors as if inviting him to take the honour of revealing their destination. Floors nodded.

"To a library," he said.

2 Alex from Mars was up to her neck in hot water and bubbles from one of the fancy designer bottles that bore names she had never heard of but assumed were upmarket brands. Any hotel/republic with the ambition of **INTERFOLD** – The Time Travel ~~Hotel~~ Republic would only stock the fanciest brands, she reasoned. Particularly on Earth, where the name on the outside of a bottle seemed so much more important than the stuff inside it. The names on the outside of bottles seemed to be the most important thing in so many people's lives, to the degree that they would work themselves ragged just to make sure that when they popped that bottle open to wash their hair in the morning, they could do so in the knowledge that they were cleansing themselves in just the right combination of petrochemical extracts of deconstructed rainforest or whatever. To her Martian senses they all smelled of the same Earth muddle and she had a hunch that it made no genuine difference which one you used.

She wondered what the Man Who Lived in a Vacuum Cleaner was doing. Probably sleeping or eating or just lying there staring at the ceiling with his surprisingly large penis in his hand, wondering what all the fuss was about. It made her mad. This Earthling obsession with ejaculating in a girl's face. She guessed somewhere, sometime there must have been an Earth government who came up with a devilish plan to bring down teenage pregnancies by convincing the young men of the world that the coolest way to get your kicks was to ice a girl's face rather than her fallopian tubes. Hire the right marketing gurus and get the message across and glued into the kids' heads with the same infectious techniques used on the branded cleansing gloop and — boom — problem solved. All you needed was control of all the usual communications channels. Whatever happened to be popular. Use it, infiltrate and manipulate and watch it work. Practise Sex Safe: Come On Her Face. She sank beneath the water and bubbles, holding her breath. Feeling the heat on her skin. Trying to clear her brain and reboot her mood.

The Man Who Lived in a Vacuum Cleaner had jumped down from the bed and run after Alex as she had slammed the bathroom door closed.

"Alex. Alex," he said, tapping at the door. "Alex?"

There was no reply. Feeling rejected, he turned and walked back towards the bed. Unlike most international hotels the accommodation within INTERFOLD was not excessively heated. As a consequence he was beginning to feel rather cold. He was also hungry. He had eaten only a tiny piece of pain aux raisins prior to the science. He knew he had made only a small dent in the side of that delicious pastry. Most of it was still on the plate. Thinking about this only made him more hungry. His stomach made a low growl of agreement.

The sound of water running came from the bathroom. Alex was drawing a bath and therefore not planning to come back out for some time. The Man Who Lived in a Vacuum Cleaner decided that, that being the case, she would not mind if he indulged in a second breakfast. He looked up at the bed. His stomach groaned again. It wanted food. It wanted pain aux raisins. Pain aux raisins was in the room going stale. Unfortunately it was going stale on a plate on a tray that was way above the Man Who Lived in a Vacuum Cleaner on Alex's bed. In his hurry to follow Alex he had given no thought in jumping down from the bed to the problem of climbing back up again.

He walked backwards away from the bed. Looking up, he could see the top of the coffee pot that stood on the tray. Beside the coffee pot he knew there was a pastry even though he could not see it.

"Work the problem," he told himself. "You can get up there; you just don't know how yet. "

He looked the bed up and down. There had to be a way. Conjuring a spontaneous plan of attack he ran at the bed and threw himself at it, jumping as high as he could and grabbing onto the draped bedclothes. This left him hanging half his height up the side of the bed, holding on to a long vertical crease in a sheet. He tried to get a purchase with his feet and climb up the crease without immediate success, but he didn't slip back down either. His grip was firm, so he took a deep breath and tried again.

"Just keep your head and your grip," he told himself, "and take it slow."

Alex from Mars came back up from under the bubbles and wiped the water from her face. Smoothed her hair back. Stood up with water cascading off her pink flesh. Looked at herself in the mirror that filled the whole wall over the double basins sunk into a marble counter opposite the bath. A simple device to make the room seem larger, she realised. She studied herself. She had lost a few kilos on Earth. She didn't know whether that was a natural adjustment to Earth gravity or whether there were just fewer calories in Earth vodka. Maybe a little of both. Her skin was a little tighter and she looked a little younger, which was odd but not unwelcome. She knew that to most Earth men she looked human. It was only when they got up close in the bedroom that the differences became obvious. The tell-tale stripes. A certain elongation of the nipples when aroused that seemed to take them by surprise. The extra orifice, lethally poisonous to Earthlings, of course. Similarly, to the untrained eye there was little obvious difference between the men of Earth and the men of Mars except, of course, that Earthmen appeared to have the smallest penises in the solar system. Apart from the Venusians. She wondered whether the closer you got to the sun the smaller the equipment, and vice versa. If she ever met a dude from Neptune she would find out.

This train of thought led her back to the Man Who Lived in a Vacuum Cleaner. If he did eventually return to regular size and his proportions remained intact he would have equipment to do a Neptunian proud. If not a Plutonian. She sucked in a deep breath and blew it out again. Maybe she would give the little guy another chance. She pulled a towel out of the rack, tossed it onto the floor and stepped out onto it, still dripping. She unlocked the door, pulled it open and stuck her head out. The Man Who Lived in a Vacuum Cleaner was sitting on the bed with a hunk of pain aux raisins in his hands, stuffing his face. Alex closed the door again. Stepped back into the bath and slid back under the water, telling herself that men were men no matter what planet they came from and if they weren't thinking with their balls they were thinking with their stomachs.

3 "Are we really going to a library?" Black asked for around the fifth time as Charon steered the boat alongside a pier jutting out from a small island that was shaped like a Spanish *sombrero cordobés* hat.

"Yes. A library," confirmed the Man Who Fell Through Floors.

"Seriously?"

"Of course."

"One hundred percent," Moe added.

"You have led me to this hat-shaped island in the middle of an underground lake—"

"Cistern," the Man Who Fell Through Floors said.

"OK, cistern, in order to take me to a library. I thought

you said you were trying to help me with a diverting excursion or idea-generating something."

"We were and we are," Moe said, "but a little subterfuge seemed to be called for given the circumstances."

"The circumstances?"

"Yes, given the circumstances. For one thing, had we told you we wanted to take you to a small hat-shaped island in an underground cistern, you would have very likely declined our help."

"And for another," the Man Who Fell Through Floors said, "had you been questioned en route you would have had no idea where we were going and thus avoided any unwelcome repercussions."

"Unwelcome repercussions?"

"Yes. Unwelcome repercussions."

"From whom?"

"The Interfold authorities, of course. They have had you followed the whole time you have been in Interfold — The Time Travel ~~Hotel~~ Republic."

"We assumed you knew," Moe said.

"Well, I had my suspicions," Black lied.

"There we are, then," the Man Who Fell Through Floors said. "Shall we go ashore?"

Black followed them in stepping out of the boat and onto the low pier. Charon sat down inside the boat to wait, patting his pockets before sighing dramatically at finding them empty. Black dipped a hand in his own pocket and threw him the Gitanes. Charon caught them and grinned a toothless smile. He tapped a cigarette out of the box, wedged it between his lips and, shielding it with cupped hands, lit it, sucking and puffing with satisfaction. Black followed the Man Who Fell Through Floors and Dave onto land, albeit a small rocky lump of land that did not look to Black as if it contained very much at all, never mind a library.

"But seriously, guys," Black said, "a library! What are we going to do? Look up in some dusty old encyclopaedia the whereabouts of a man who may or may not be known under the name Eugenides? Even if we did, how would we know whether the Eugenides referred to was, is or will one day be the same Eugenides that I have been sent to Interfold to locate?" He shook his head, waving his hands about as he spoke, frustrated as he saw another day evaporate in fruitless activity.

"Look, Black," the Man Who Fell Through Floors said, "for one thing, we are not just taking you to any old library. We are taking you to one of the most secret libraries on the planet. A library that contains a unique store of ancient knowledge including the majority of the lost library of Mattias Corvinus, looted from Budapest in 1541 and lost somewhere in Constantinople-Istanbul until looted again along with this cistern by Interfold — The Time Travel ~~Hotel~~ Republic."

"Which is all very interesting," Black said, "and were I here as a tourist I would be fascinated, but I am not. I need to make some progress in establishing whether this man remains in Interfold and I fail to see how a bunch of ancient books is going to help me."

"Black, buddy," Moe said, "we haven't bought you here for the books or even for the library."

"But you said—"

"I know, I know," Dave said. "Let me explain. We have bought you here to see the librarian who looks after the library, rather than the library itself."

"The librarian?" Black asked.

"Yes, the librarian," the Man Who Fell Through Floors agreed.

"And you have brought me here to see him?"

"Absolutely."

"And how exactly is that better?" Black asked. "Does he have a unique insight into the whereabouts of all men known by the name of Eugenides?"

"Not all of them and not necessarily the one you seek, but he has been known to quote the name."

"He has?"

"He has. Although..." Moe paused.

"Yes?"

"Not since 1922."

"1922?"

"Yes. 1922," the Man Who Fell Through Floors said.

"Who on Earth is he?" Black asked.

"T.S. Eliot," Moe answered.

4 The Dwarf with the Horse, Pedro and three ASSIIR agents were wedged together in a typically INTERFOLDian service elevator somewhere in the north-north-eastern corner of **INTERFOLD**. It was too small for the occupants to fit comfortably, was old and slow, and, for a reason best known to the **INTERFOLD** Vertical Transportation Maintenance Authority, was painted pink.

"I am **NOT** happy. I am **NOT** happy. I am **NOT** happy," Pedro was saying over and over and over again. The Dwarf was gently stroking the highest point on Pedro's shoulder that he could reach and doing what he could to keep his companion calm.

"Not much longer, not much longer, just keep calm, just keep calm," he said.

"I thought it was stairs he doesn't like," Agent No. 1 said.

"Yeah," said the Dwarf, "but he gets claustrophobic as well."

"A claustrophobic horse!" ASSIIR Agent No. 3 laughed. He was wedged between Pedro's haunch and the back wall of the elevator. An elevator that, with a horse, a dwarf and three men in it, was jammed tight. The agent's arms were pinned by his sides and as he laughed Pedro exerted a subtle pressure against him.

"Stop it!" the agent squeaked.

"What did he say?" Pedro asked the Dwarf.

"I have no idea." The Dwarf grinned.

"Maybe one of his girlfriends will translate."

"You never know!"

"Stop whatever you are doing, horse," Agent No. 2 said to Pedro.

"Me? I am just standing here trying to keep calm," Pedro said.

"Arrrrgggghhhhhh," said the agent he was crushing against the wall.

"Make him stop!" Agent No. 1 said to the Dwarf.

"I thought you kids would have worked out by now that Pedro does just about what he pleases. I have very little influence, you know," the Dwarf said calmly, watching the old analogue display count through the floors as they descended.

"Arrrrrrgggghhhhh," squealed the crushed agent again.

Pedro chuckled and flicked his tail in the face of the agent just to make his point, then relented and eased the pressure on the agent so that he could breathe.

"I am a *horse*," he said, "bred from a noble line of stallions. Elevators are not my natural habitat and are only marginally preferable to stairs." He re-applied the pressure.

"Arrrrrrgggggghhhhh!" the ASSIIR agent wailed.

"What floor are we meant to be heading for?" the Dwarf asked the other agents as their colleague moaned.

"The basement," Agent No. 1 said.

"Minus one on the elevator scale," Agent No. 2 clarified.

"Make him stoooopppp!" Agent No. 3 moaned.

"I thought so," the Dwarf said.

"And your point is?" Agent No. 1 asked.

"Not a point so much as an observation," the Dwarf said.

"Yes?" said Agent No. 2.

The Dwarf turned his head and looked up at the agent. "That there is no minus one showing on the display. It goes down, blah, blah, blah, five, four, three, two, one, Ground, Parking."

"Parking?" Agent No. 2 said, looking up at the display. "Are you sure it says Parking?"

"Well, it is marked with a P," the Dwarf said. "That would mean 'parking' in most of the hotels and resorts that Pedro and I have stayed in over the years."

"That may be so," Agent No. 1 said.

"But this is Interfold," Agent No. 2 added.

"Oooooooh," Agent No. 3 moaned. He had gone blue and his eyes were half-closed. The Dwarf ducked under Pedro and peered up at the agent.

"Maybe you should let him alone now, Pedro," he said. "I think he has learned his lesson."

"Are you sure?" Pedro asked.

"Yes. He has gone blue. I think we are in enough trouble already. How do you think that woman will react if she hears you killed one of the guards in an elevator?"

"Good point, buddy," Pedro said, and he shifted his weight to let the agent breathe.

"Th-th-thank... you," he gasped, "not... not... par... par... not..."

"What?" Agent No. 1 asked him.

"Not... park... parking."

"Not parking?" Agent No. 2 said.

"No," Agent No. 3 panted, catching his breath. "No parking in Interfold. Not permitted."

"I think the dude is delirious," the Dwarf said.

Pedro chuckled. "Reminds me of a girl."

"Yeah?" the Dwarf said. "Which one?"

"Dolores," Pedro said. "I honestly thought her name was Delirious."

"Delirious Dolores," the Dwarf said, smiling warmly at the memory. "Wow... I had forgotten all about her." He whistled. "She really was something. I could have settled down with her."

"Tell me about it," Pedro said. "She was a one-off. They don't build 'em like Dolores any more."

"I know what you mean," the Dwarf said, nodding.

"Farm girl," Pedro said.

"She certainly knew her way around the livestock," the Dwarf said, grinning.

"Watch it, buddy!" Pedro said. "The livestock here does not appreciate being referred to as livestock."

The Dwarf laughed. The ASSIIR agents ignored them and stared at the analogue display in concern as it ticked oh-so-slowly down through five... four... three... two... one... Ground... and finally to P.

5 "T.S. Eliot," Black said. "But isn't he dead?"

"No more than Elvis," the Man Who Fell Through Floors said.

"Elvis?"

"Yes. Elvis. Elvis Presley."

"But he is dead, and so is T.S. Eliot."

"Shhh, not so loud, Black," Dave cut in. "That may be so, but neither T.S. nor Elvis knows that they are dead, so it is really not polite to bring it up."

"What?"

"Neither of them is aware that in the contemporary timeline that Interfold is currently aligned with, they are both in fact dead. So it really is best if you don't mention it to either T.S. or Elvis, should you bump into him."

"Bump into him? You mean Elvis Presley really is here in Interfold? That's amazing. Am I likely to bump into him?"

"No," the Man Who Fell Through Floors said. "He is a master of disguise. Ah, here we are."

They had arrived at the top of some steps that cut down through the earth to a door. It looked like the entrance to a long-barrow, only the door was blue and had a large brass knocker and letterbox and the steps that descended to it were made from books: marble books, but books all the same. Black followed his companions down the steps and watched as the Man Who Fell Through Floors knocked on the door.

They waited. After a few minutes the Man Who Fell Through Floors knocked again and the door immediately opened a few inches to reveal T.S. Eliot as he would have looked, looks or will look during the early 1920s. They all looked at him, confused.

"Yes," he said, "can I help you?"

"Mr Eliot?" the Man Who Fell Through Floors enquired.

"Yes."

"Mr T.S. Eliot?"

"Yes."

"Mr T.S. Eliot the poet, writer of *The Waste Land*?"

"How do you know that?"

"Know what?" the Man Who Fell Through Floors asked.

"That I am working on something I have considered calling *The Waste Land*."

The Man Who Fell Through Floors looked at Dave as realisation dropped into his train of thought and clarified the delicacy of the situation.

"Interfold is rife with rumours, you know," he said. "Nothing stays confidential for long. Even if you are down here on the lake."

"Cistern," Moe said.

"Or even cistern."

"That aside," T.S. Eliot said, "what is it that I can do for you?"

"Our friend here is looking for someone and we thought you might be able to assist," Moe said, gesturing to Black. T.S. Eliot looked at Black and sighed.

"Come in and I will see what I can do to help." He stood back and held the door as Black, the Man Who Fell Through Floors and Moe stepped into the library. T.S. Eliot closed the door and walked past them to lead the way between bookshelves and piles of books to his small office. He moved more books out of the way and cleared three chairs, before taking a seat himself behind a glass-topped desk. A red analogue telephone with a finger wheel sat on the desk between neat, meticulously arranged piles of papers and yet more books. It began to ring. T.S. Eliot picked up the receiver, said, "T.S. Eliot," and immediately hung up.

"Rather annoying," he said. "Who is this person you are looking for?"

"Eugenides," said Black.

"Eugenides?"

"Yes. Eugenides."

"Just Eugenides? No other name? No initial."

"No. That is all I have to go on."

"Eugenides, eh?" T.S. Eliot said, picking up a fountain pen and writing the name on a notepad. "Never heard of him."

"What?" the Man Who Fell Through Floors asked. "But—"

"Can you offer any suggestions," Moe cut in, "that might help us help our friend here in taking a step or two in the right direction? Any methodologies or terms of reference that might aid his enquiries?"

"Me?" T.S. Eliot asked. "You are aware that I am a poet and a banker?"

"Yes."

"I am surprised that either is reason enough for you to consider me a trustworthy source of information."

"It was just a hunch, I guess," Dave said.

"And..." the Man Who Fell Through Floors began.

"Yes?"

"...we thought maybe the library might have some records, some ledgers, legal documentation..." He looked round at Dave and Black for assistance.

"Yes," Moe said, "like a register of guests, residents and citizens of Interfold — The Time Travel Hotel Republic."

"You really thought that the authorities would keep those kinds of records down here?" T.S. Eliot asked Black.

"Hey, don't ask me, buddy," Black said. "I thought I was going fishing until about twenty minutes ago."

"Fishing?" T.S. Eliot said.

"Yes," Black said, "fishing. Although that turned out to be a deliberate deception to keep the Feds off my tail."

"The Feds?"

"Yes, the Feds."

"Off your tail?"

"Yes, off my tail."

"I have not the faintest idea what this man is talking about," T.S. Eliot said to the Man Who Fell Through Floors and Moe.

At that moment Charon came striding in jabbering in Greek, gesticulating and pointing back towards the door. T.S. Eliot stood up and went to him. A hurried exchange conducted entirely in Greek followed. When it stopped Charon rushed back outside. T.S. Eliot turned to his three visitors and looked from one to the other in turn.

"Your boatman wanted to warn you that someone called Dixon and the, ahem, Feds, whoever they may be, are almost here and that he is off as he cannot afford a confrontation with the authorities. He says you have one minute to join him."

Black leapt to his feet, followed closely by the Man Who Fell Through Floors and Moe.

"Is there another way out?" Black asked, thinking that he had no desire to reveal his lack of progress to the Dragon Lady's chief henchman.

"Another way out?"

"Yes. Another way out."

"There is something I am told is an emergency exit, although I have never used it myself."

"You had better show us where it is."

T.S. Eliot considered the situation and then nodded.

"OK," he said, "follow me."

"Wait, Black," the Man Who Fell Through Floors said. "You take the emergency exit and Moe and I will go with Charon. Hopefully they will follow us and that will throw them off your trail."

"Good plan," Black agreed. "Good luck, guys. Mr Eliot, lead the way."

6 As the elevator stopped with the analogue display illuminating the letter P in electric blue, the ASSIIR agent who had been squeezed against the wall of the elevator by Pedro finally regained enough breath to say:

"What I mean is that, as parking is not permitted in Interfold — The Time Travel ~~Hotel~~ Republic, the P does not indicate parking but..."

Before he could finish the voice of a disembodied, female(ish) English speaker who was not of English origin — indeed, judging by the excessively nasal intonation, most probably not from Earth but from a planet where it was usual to have a greater number of nasal cavities than was, is or may well always be the regular number of nasal cavities for an Earthling — announced:

"Atmospheric support conditions mammalian Earthlings for, will present be shortly. We for this short delay do apologise."

"Does she mean me?" Pedro asked. "Mammalian? Or you, shorty?"

"I think she means all of us, buddy, don't worry," the Dwarf said.

"...Plurality," Agent No. 3 said.

"What?" the first of his colleagues asked.

"Plurality," Agent No. 3 said again. "Because Interfold exists on the edge of a dimensional fracture, there are parts of the Interfold complex that are categorised as Pluralities because it is statistically more likely in those locations that you will find yourself in a time, place, dimension or universe other than the one you expected to find yourself in. Hence it is very unlikely that when the doors open we will find ourselves in a..."

Before he could finish the doors opened to reveal row upon row of cars in a brightly illuminated, clinically clean and white concrete...

"...parking lot."

"Looks like a parking lot to me," the Dwarf said.

"Yep," Pedro agreed, "me too."

"Whooooaaaa," ASSIIR Agent No. 2 said, walking out into the parking lot and looking around. "You know where this is?"

"No," Pedro said, following and looking along the row of cars bisected by the concrete shaft that contained their elevator. Stretching off into the distance he could see an infinite number of vehicles. He looked the other way, which looked exactly the same. If he looked over the row of cars opposite he could see an infinite number of rows of cars as far as he could see.

"This," the agent continued, "is the Car Park at Infinity." He looked at his four companions, expecting to see their faces as awed as his own. He was disappointed.

"The what?" the Dwarf asked.

"The Car Park at Infinity."

"Do you know what this one is on about?" the Dwarf asked Pedro.

"Yep," Pedro said.

"What?" the Dwarf exclaimed. "Really?"

"Of course," Pedro said. "It is to do with Rodriguez's third theory of infinity. The first two were really only warm-ups, but it was the third that really made the money."

"Rodriguez's third theory?" the Dwarf said, grinning.

"Yeah," Pedro said. "It states that infinity is where all possible points in all possible universes meet."

"I am impressed, Pedro."

"Thanks. Smart boy, that Rodriguez, though."

"Sounds like it."

"Not only does he coin one of the definitive theories of infinity, but he goes on to hypothesise that if infinity is indeed the point where all possible points in all possible universes meet, then..."

"Yes?"

"There will need to be one hell of a lot of parking."

"And you think that this is the parking lot?"

"Sure. Why not? He cleaned up, you know."

"Rodriguez?"

"Yep. One smart cookie."

"So you think this is the Car Park at Infinity?"

"Could be. It looks pretty big."

"You're not wrong. Look at all these cars."

"If this is the Car Park at Infinity," Agent No. 2 said, "I have heard that not only does it contain enough parking for an infinite number of cars but at any one moment it will contain every car ever conceived in any conceivable universe."

"Any car at all?" the Dwarf asked.

"Quite a concept," Pedro said, walking along the row of cars. The Dwarf followed, looking at the row opposite to Pedro.

"Hey, buddy," he said, "check this out."

Pedro turned and walked back and stopped beside the Dwarf. "What am I looking at?" he asked, looking at a metallic gold coupé.

"Look at the emblem on the grille."

"What about it?"

"It is a horse."

"So?"

"You are a horse."

"So I am," Pedro said, "and your point is?"

"You would never fit in there!"

"Good point, but that would be true of most of these vehicles."

"It's a Mustang," Agent No. 2 said, joining them. His two companions had walked on ahead, looking for a way out.

"A Mustang?" Pedro echoed. "I have not heard of that one before. Where is it from?"

"It's American."

"American? You're kidding. It doesn't look like one of those crazy American cars."

"What do you mean?"

"You know," the Dwarf said, "all American cars are poky little boxy things. Worst cars ever built. All the best cars are Russian. Everybody knows that."

"Except those monster limousines the American big guns get driven about in," Pedro said.

"Yeah, except those. Only good thing to ever come out of APAC."

"What is APAC?" the agent asked.

"The American People's Automotive Collective," the Dwarf said. "Only ever produced two things that were any good: huge limousines and Chairwoman River Like a Churning Hurricane."

"What are you two talking about?" the agent asked. "You have it all the wrong way round. American cars are big, cool, gas-guzzling, beefy hunks of metal. Russian cars are a joke."

"Not where we come from," Pedro said.

"And we know of what we speak, dude," the Dwarf said. "We spent some quality time with the chairwoman in question, doing a little celebrating in the back of one of those limos the night she became President of the USSA after a quiet little coup d'état that we may or may not have had a little hand in staging."

"The USSA?"

"Yep. The United Soviet States of America. Finest workers' republic in history," Pedro said, "where all sentient creatures are considered equal. Unlike this would-be republic of Interblown or whatever you call it."

"There is no such country," the ASSIIR agent said. "You have it all wrong."

"Oh, yeah?" Pedro asked. "And how many talking horses are there in your dimension?"

"Right now? Just the one."

"And before today?"

"None."

"Do the math, kiddo, do the math," Pedro said, and he

walked on down the line of cars.

The other two ASSIIR agents were a way ahead of the three when the air immediately in front of them began to shimmer and a tall and slender, bright blue, vaguely humanoid being materialised. It stood motionless for a moment as Pedro and the others joined the two agents.

"Apologies," it said in polite electronic English, and it disappeared in a shimmer only to reappear almost immediately in the form of a centaur.

"I think it is attempting to appear to us in a form that we will find familiar," ASSIIR Agent No. 1 said, "although the presence of the Horse appears to be confusing it."

"Please stand still. Scanning for identification and vehicle retrieval."

There was a pause. No one moved.

"Scan negative. Re-scanning."

A further pause was characterised by a similar lack of movement.

"Scan negative. We regret that your vehicle or vehicles are not currently parked within our facilities. You have one minute to exit via the nearest Earthling-friendly disembarkation point before atmospheric conditions are returned to gravity vacuum quality seven. You have not been charged for this service. Thank you for visiting the Car Park at Infinity." The blue centaur disappeared with a sound that might best be described as an excessively polite butler, with a vaguely Quebecois accent, saying *ciao* in what he thinks is an alluring whisper.

"What was that all about?" the Dwarf asked.

"I think," said ASSIIR Agent No. 2, "that it means we had better get back to the elevator."

"And it might be best if we don't hang around," ASSIIR Agent No. 1 said.

"In fact," ASSIIR Agent No. 3 added, "you might want to run."

They all looked at each other for a stupid frozen moment and then all five dashed back along the row of cars to the elevator.

"What has happened?" ASSIIR Agent No. 2 asked as he arrived a second behind the others to find, as they had, that the elevator door was no longer present but had been replaced by a wooden door with a frosted glass panel in it. An orange light glowed through the glass and a vaguely visible form shifted slightly within. A carved wooden sign over the door had the word "SAUNA" burnt into it.

"Open the door," Agent No. 3 said. "It is just an anomaly."

"You open the door," Agent No. 1 said.

"Don't worry, girls," the Dwarf said, "I will open the door." He stepped forward and pulled the door open to reveal a sauna.

"It looks like a sauna," Pedro said.

"Where has the elevator gone?" ASSIIR Agent No. 1 asked, looking like he had been slapped with a couple of wet hake.

"Do you want to explain or shall I?" Pedro asked Agent No. 3.

"I really don't think we have time," ASSIIR Agent No. 3 said. "We just need to get inside the sauna before the atmosphere resets and we suffocate."

"Good point," the Dwarf said. He stepped forward, but as he did a very red, very naked Black McCarthy staggered out of the sauna and bent over, panting, his right hand on the shoulder of the Dwarf and his left arm held across his body with his left hand holding his ribs as he gasped.

"Thanks," he said. "Damn thing... was locked... and... wouldn't open... from the inside." Black looked rough. Blood was crusted around his nostrils and his left ear. A red swelling over his right eye, the way he was holding his ribs and a red boot-print-shaped welt on his abdomen indicated he had been given a good going-over. "Where is... Joylin?" he asked.

"No idea, dude," the Dwarf said. "No one here by the name of Joylin... unless he means one of you three?"

"Don't get lippy, Dwarf," Agent No. 1 said as Pedro chuckled.

"What happened to you, man?" Pedro asked Black. "You look rough. Not to mention... kinda naked. Where are your clothes?"

"Long story," Black panted.

"Excuse me for interrupting, but I really think we all need to get into the sauna as quickly as possible," ASSIIR Agent No. 3 said. "The atmosphere in here will become deadly any second now."

"No way..." Black said, sagging almost to his knees, "can't... go... back... in... there... too... hot." He pushed himself upright and limped away from the Dwarf with the Horse, Pedro and the three agents in the direction of the space where the blue parking attendant had appeared. As he approached the same point the air shimmered as before and this time a naked blue female humanoid appeared.

"Why, Mr McCarthy," she said with a soft Irish lilt that sounded somewhat like a girl from Nantes who had learned English in Kilkenny. "How good to see you. Your vehicle will be with you momentarily. Please attend."

The others came up behind Black and watched as the sound of an engine grew from away in the distance until it materialised into the form of a white 2025-model Land Rover Electrolite-Zakhele 22-7 which, due to a fashion for retro styling, looked rather like it always did, does or most certainly will look in a dealership near you at some point. The Land Rover reversed towards them at great speed with tyres smoking; it stopped half a metre from Black and all five doors sprang open. Black stepped round the car and slid carefully into the driver's seat. He was about to pull the door closed when he leant back out and called to the Dwarf with the Horse, Pedro and the three ASSIIR agents:

"Are you coming or are you going to take your chances in that sauna?"

The Dwarf, Pedro and the agents all rushed forward. The Dwarf jumped in the back and threw down the seats. Pedro struggled into the back after him, kneeling down. The agents all piled in and knelt beside Pedro as the Dwarf climbed forward into the front passenger seat.

"Ready when you are," he said to McCarthy.

Black, still hunched and listing to his left, his left arm now hanging awkwardly at his side, looked down at him. "Do you think you can put that in drive for me?" He nodded down at the gear shift.

"Sure thing," the Dwarf said, and he did as he was asked. Black gripped the steering wheel with his right hand and hit the gas, tearing away down between the rows of cars.

"Do you know where you are going?" ASSIIR Agent No. 3 asked.

"Of course," Black said. "I have been here before."

"Exit approaching in five — four — three — two — one — zero," the voice of the blue female humanoid announced.

"Hold on," Black said, "here we go." A portion of the concrete floor dropped away in a haze of blue-white light and Black drove down into it, accelerating. "You need to pick up some speed for a smooth exit," he explained.

They continued down as the speedometer showed the Land Rover rising to 80 mph. The light grew around them and they had the sense that the floor was starting to rise. Black frowning as he peered into the light, keeping the needle on 80 mph, which he recalled as the optimum speed for exit momentum. "Almost there," he said, and they shot up above ground and right into the mayhem of downtown city traffic.

Black swerved to avoid a slow-moving truck, hit the brake to bring the speed of the Land Rover down, slipped in front of the truck and said, "Not bad. Last time was a total write-off. Anyone know where we are?"

"Nope," the Dwarf said.

"Phnom Penh, most likely," ASSIIR Agent No. 3 said. "That is where Interfold was located when we entered the elevator. But given that we entered the Car Park via a Plurality we could be anywhere."

"OK," Black said, looking ahead and scanning the skyline, "let's assume Phnom Penh. Can anyone see Interfold from here?"

They all craned around, looking out of various windows without success.

"We could try the navigation system, I suppose," Black said. "Julia?"

"Yes, Mr McCarthy," the voice of a posh English girl answered.

"Can you get us to INTERFOLD, assuming it is still here, and is *here* Phnom Penh?"

"One moment," Julia replied, "I am connecting with the Martian satellites. This being February 1996 there are as yet no reliable public navigation satellites available. I could hack into the US military system, but you know how ropey their technology is."

"For sure," Black answered, and to the Dwarf and co. he added, "Martian Red 27 Trajectory Plus: best navigation systems in the solar system, you know."

"So I have heard," Pedro answered. "Does this one have the multiple personality provider upgrade?"

"Sure does."

"Nice," Pedro said, nodding in approval.

"Only it seems to have become stuck on Vicar's Daughter," Black said.

"Very nice," Pedro added, to the amusement of the Dwarf.

"Connection complete. Interfold — The Time Travel Hotel

Republic located in Phnom Penh, Cambodia, Earth. As are you. Time scan suggests you have only around a further ten hours before it completes its next time shift."

"Should be long enough."

"Indeed it will," Julia told him. "Stay in this lane and turn left at the next junction, or would you rather I take the wheel? You do have a tendency to miss time-critical manoeuvres."

"Good with me, Julia. Switch to autopilot confirmed." Black took his hand off the steering wheel and his foot off the gas and turned his head to the Dwarf. "Don't you just love technology?"

"Sure, dude," the Dwarf said, adjusting his shades and putting his feet up on the dashboard, "whatever."

7 The Man Who Lived in a Vacuum Cleaner had been partially forgiven. Alex from Mars had relented and let him into the bathroom. She had sat him on a towel curled into a nest on the marble counter beside the basins. Alex herself had returned to the bath, having refreshed the water and the bubbling gloop.

"Are there many of you here on Earth?" the Man Who Lived in a Vacuum Cleaner asked.

"I don't know," Alex said. "Not about Earth, anyway."

"What about other planets?"

"Oh, we travel about; I think you might find the odd Martian all over the place. I am not the best person to ask, though."

"Why not?"

"I haven't been anywhere but Interfold, wherever that is. So I can't really say what the other planets are like. Aside from the convention that we are not meant to interfere on Earth, I am not very knowledgeable about that sort of thing."

"Convention?"

"It is something to do with letting primitive planets develop at their own pace. The other planets go to great lengths to make it look like no one is out there so that you guys can find your own way."

"That is amazing."

"It wasn't always like that. I remember when I was a kid there was this comedy show dressed up as documentary about life on Earth. It was a massive hit, really popular, but a lot of people thought it was wrong to laugh at you all just because you were on a slower developmental curve and eventually it was taken off air."

"I had never thought of Earth as primitive."

"It is all a matter of perspective. You would probably look at some of the things we think of as normal and think the same. I certainly do."

"So are there civilisations on all eight planets?" the Man Who Lived in a Vacuum Cleaner asked.

"Fourteen."

"Fourteen?"

"Yes, fourteen. Some are shielded so that they can't be seen from Earth."

"Why?"

"Because they are ostentatious technology knob wavers. On Mars we just beam an image of the planet that is three hundred and seventy-five thousand years old so that you think it is empty, and every time you send one of your little robot things we divert it into the desert and leave interesting rocks around for it to find."

"Are we sending robots to Mars?"

"Uh-huh."

"I had no idea. That is amazing."

"Really?"

"I think so."

"It is broadcast as a comedy show on Mars. Or was. I think it may have been banned now. Even we make progress from time to time."

"How do the robots get to Mars? Do we use balloons?"

"Balloons?" Alex said with a small snort of laughter. "No, with rockets."

"Rockets?" the Man Who Lived in a Vacuum Cleaner asked. "Robots. Rockets. This is the sort of thing that writers and movie studios make up. We didn't have rockets or robots back when I am from."

"Really?" Alex from Mars asked. "I forget that you guys have been on technological fast-forward for the last Earth century I was on Mars. I guess I must be a few decades ahead of you. Of course you would need to stay on that course for another six or seven hundred years to get anywhere near us."

"Really?"

"For sure. But we were launching our first interplanetary missions when you guys were still painting yourselves blue and dancing around naked in stone circles."

"Not all of us. My people would have been at the high end of Earth civilisation at that time."

"Really? I can believe that." Alex stood up. "Time to get out, I think." Water cascaded off her in what seemed to the Man Who Lived in a Vacuum Cleaner to be a sparkling waterfall. She pulled her hair back behind her head with both hands and squeezed. He stared at her body, mesmerised. The surprisingly large penis did what surprisingly large penises are supposed to do and rose to the occasion to give Alex from Mars a salute from Earth.

"Could I have that towel?" Alex asked. "This one is wet." She stepped out of the bath as the Man Who Lived in a Vacuum Cleaner stood up to step out of the towel. The rush of blood to his saluting penis once more left him woozy and he swayed as he tried to disentangle himself from the towel.

And then everything went all fast-forward-crazy. Alex slipped on the wet floor. The Man Who Lived in a Vacuum Cleaner stumbled on the counter with his foot trapped in the towel. Alex fell towards him. He started to fall towards the edge of the counter. Alex reached out a desperate arm; whether to stop herself falling or to stop him she would not afterwards be able to say. Her outstretched hand missed him and missed the counter but caught the very edge of the towel, pulling it down with her as she fell. The Man Who Lived in a Vacuum Cleaner was flipped off the counter as the towel was whipped away from under him, throwing him up into the air. He sailed past Alex as she hit the floor and he started to fall towards the toilet. Alex tried to turn and get up fast enough to save him, but it was too late. He plummeted towards the open toilet, bouncing off the chrome handle as he fell. The toilet began to flush in a white whirlpool of INTERFOLD plumbing fury into which the Man Who Lived in a Vacuum Cleaner disappeared. Alex rolled over, pushed herself up and plunged a hand into the toilet to save him, but she was too late. He was gone.

8 Julia steered the Land Rover Electrolite-Zakhele 22-7 across town towards **INTERFOLD** — The Time Travel ~~Hotel~~ Republic where it had taken up residence on the banks of the Mekong. Black sat back and left the driving to the technology.

"So you are like a detective?" the Dwarf asked.

"After a fashion," Black said.

"So what is the most gruesome case you have worked on?"

"There haven't been that many."

"You must have seen some stuff, though, the crazy scrapes people get themselves into."

"For sure," Black said, "but that is not really my speciality."

"Bet you've solved a bunch of tricky cases though, eh?"

"I guess you could say... a number," Black said, not wanting to commit himself.

"Must be great, though," the Dwarf went on. "Me and Pedro love a good 'tec movie, don't we, Pedro?"

"Sure thing," Pedro said.

"The sleuth tracking down the crook. Taking the blows. In and out of the shadows."

"Getting the girl," Pedro said.

"Yeah, getting the girl, you dudes always get the girl!"

"The reality is much less interesting," Black said.

"Oh, yeah?" the Dwarf said, looking the naked and bruised Black up and down. "Sure. Whatever you say. But you look like you are into something. What about that girl you mentioned? What was her name?"

"Joylin," Pedro said.

"Yeah, man, Joylin. What about Joylin? Does she live up to her name?"

"What he means is," Pedro said, "is she hot?"

"Oh, for goodness sake!" the Wolf said, materialising in the passenger seat, displacing the Dwarf, who was alarmed to find himself relocated into the back and squeezed in with Pedro and the three **ASSIIR** agents. "Every time I check in you are discussing some woman rather than focusing on the job at hand, McCarthy. It makes me wonder whether I made a mistake in hiring you."

"Give me a break, Wolf; do I look like I am shirking?"

"Ha, maybe; maybe not. It can be so very hard to tell. But what news do you have for me?"

"He is still in Interfold."

"He is, is he? That is good news."

"It wasn't easy information to come by, as I think you can tell by my appearance."

"That, McCarthy, is what we pay you for. If it was easy I wouldn't need you, would I?"

"I guess not."

"And what of that girl you were talking about?" the Wolf asked. "Joylin, was it?"

"Alive, the last I saw of her."

"And Dixon?"

"Dead."

"Dead?"

"Yes, dead."

"Ah. So it goes. Who killed him? Was it this... Joylin?"

"Joylin?"

"Yes, Joylin."

"No."

"You?" the Wolf asked, more than a little surprised. "Well, well, McCarthy, you have more about you than meets the eye."

"Yep," Black said.

"Although it is unfortunate," the Wolf said, "and likely to draw unwanted attention."

"But necessary," Black said. "It was me or him."

"Did he reveal anything?"

"No," Black said. He laughed. "Nor was he likely to, no matter what we had to offer. He'd have bled me dry and killed Joylin. I had no choice."

"Weapon?"

"Pistol."

"The one Joylin gave you?"

"No." Black thought about this for a long moment before saying, "How did you know about that?"

"I have my methods," the Wolf said. "What next?"

"Back to Interfold and continue my research. I have some further leads to follow up, assuming we are going back into Interfold at about the same time we left. Julia?"

"You were last seen visiting Mr T.S. Eliot and are returning later that day," Julia said in her very nice English accent.

"What?" Black asked. "That was weeks ago!"

"Not to worry, McCarthy," the Wolf said. "Perhaps this will give you the chance to gain from some missed opportunities.

Go back over some ground. See what you missed."

"Does that mean Dixon is still alive on this timeline?"

"No," Julia replied, "you killed him this morning. Here we are; shall I pull up before or will you go through security?"

"Go through security," the Wolf said. "I will deal with them."

Julia steered the car up to a temporary security barrier that had been erected by the Cambodian authorities in the fence they had hastily slung around the perimeter of INTERFOLD — The Time Travel ~~Hotel~~ Republic. She pulled up at the security barrier and automatically rolled down the front windows on both sides of the car.

"Permits and ID," a weary Cambodian asked in English, as a companion lounged in the doorway of their guard hut, an automatic rifle resting in his arms.

"You can go about your business," the Wolf said.

"You can go about your business," the guard repeated.

"Please proceed through the barrier," the Wolf continued.

"Please proceed through the barrier," said the guard.

"This is not the horse we are looking for."

"This is not the horse we are looking for," the guard told his companion, gesturing for him to raise the barrier.

"Have a good day, sir," the Wolf added.

"Have a good day, sir," the guard said, and he saluted as Julia rolled the windows back up and proceeded towards the main entrance to INTERFOLD.

"I have always wanted to do that," the Wolf said, "ever since I saw *Star Wars* as a kid. Brilliant."

Black ignored him and unclipped his seatbelt as Julia pulled to a halt at the bottom of the steps to the main door into INTERFOLD.

"Off you go, McCarthy," the Wolf said. "I shall see that the car is returned to the Car Park at Infinity. Be sure to summon me if there is anything to report."

"Of course," Black said, "of course." He stepped out of the car and strolled up the steps back into INTERFOLD wearing nothing but his old Converse sneakers. The left one green, the right one red.

9 The Girl with Nine Lives was standing on one leg on the stage in the Red Light Basement. She was standing on one leg because the other had been removed below the knee by the expert surgical hands of Doctor Klown as instructed by the INTERFOLD Immigration adjudication. It had of course healed over in minutes and thus she had been judged ready to complete the other part of her sentence in the form of servitude in the Red Light Basement.

Walter and His Softy Chums were as usual laying down their trademark lazy blues, against which the Girl with Nine Lives understood she was expected to disrobe. This was easier than she had anticipated it would be on two counts. The first because the lights were very bright and the audience, few though they were in number, were no more than hazy silhouettes. The second because she was still wearing nothing more than the surgical gown she had been given by Doctor Klown that morning, whenever that was, is or one day will be. As such, letting the gown fall to the floor proved less distressing than it might have been. What she was meant to do after that she had no idea, so she simply concentrated on balancing on her one good leg as Walter crunched to an indifferent halt and the lights came up to reveal Black McCarthy, the Dwarf, Pedro and the three ASSIIR agents staring at her from the bar. She froze for a moment, feeling weak, and then relaxed and with a deep breath and a smile hopped off the low stage and across the room, dodging between tables. Hopping up to Black, she threw her arms around his neck and planted a big wet kiss on his cheek.

"Mr McCarthy," she said, "you absolute sweetie. You didn't have to, really you didn't. How wonderful of you to show such solidarity. I cannot begin to tell you how much this means to me."

"I — er..." Black said, having no idea what she meant. "It was nothing... just seemed like the appropriate thing to do." He flushed, embarrassed less by his lack of understanding than by the sudden increasing weight he felt in his loins as a volume of blood headed in that direction; the Girl with Nine Lives's breasts brushed against him as she hugged him tighter and whispered in his ear.

"Do you think you could do me one more favour?"

"Of course," Black said. He tried to cough away his embarrassment.

"I am rather expected to... you know... leave with a

customer, if you take my meaning." She gestured with her eyes to a round American wearing a bow tie and small round glasses who was loitering close at hand, mopping his brow with a red bandana.

"Of course," Black said. "Hey, buddy, get lost. The lady is spoken for."

Crestfallen, the round American returned to his table at the front of the stage.

"Thank you."

"No problem at all."

"It would rather help, though, if we could leave and perhaps go to your room."

"My room?"

"Yes, your room. It really would be a great help. Just for tonight."

"I see," Black said, going deeper crimson.

"And it would help stop your friends from staring at me." She tipped her head slightly in the direction of the Dwarf with the Horse and Pedro, who were both looking at Black and grinning wide "I told you so" smiles.

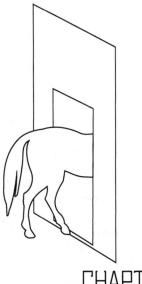

CHAPTER TWELVE

Black McCarthy was dreaming. He was dreaming a jumbled montage of recent events. Recent — to him at least — days, recent hours, jagged fragments that kept switching back into each other, folding in and over, becoming more disjointed and incoherent as the dream proceeded.

He had swept two or three times over non-sequential elements from the series of events that included his capture and interrogation by Dixon spliced with his exit from the sauna. The bungled rescue attempt by Joylin. Her capture mangled up with him leaving the Red Light Basement with the Girl with Nine Lives. The dejection he felt at the lack of sexual competence he had displayed in bed with the Nurse with the Curse. Standing over Dixon with the gun in his hand. Doctor Klown bursting into Suite 9762 just as Black and the Nurse... Joylin in his bathroom. Why was she always in his bathroom?

"Because I hadn't expected you to arrive back with a naked woman," she said. "I was waiting to see if you got back here at all."

"Of course I got back here," Black said. "I am more resourceful than you give me credit for, Joylin."

"So why the naked woman?"

"I was trying to be helpful."

"I bet you were."

"Joylin, it was genuinely an attempt at a good deed. Don't get fixated on the nakedness."

"It is rather hard not to." She looked him up and down, "Where are your clothes? The last time I saw you, you had clothes on. Was it some ridiculous drinking game with your buddies, who I take it you still have not killed for me?"

"Joylin, Joylin," Black said, putting a finger to his lips, "please keep it down. She will hear you. And no, I have not killed my employer and the Man Who Falls Through Floors and nor am I going to. I killed one man for you. Is that not enough?"

"Humph," Joylin said, folding her arms across her chest, "I suppose it might be. Although..."

"Yes?"

"He was almost unconscious."

"Which you handled rather brilliantly."

"Yes, I know. Did you really need to shoot him?"

"Yes."

"Oh."

"Dead men don't talk, Joylin."

"I suppose not."

"I had no choice."

"I see that, but..."

"Yes?"

"Where does that leave us now?"

"I am guessing that Dixon was off-piste when he locked me up, and I hope that this will buy me some time."

"Time enough?"

"I reckon so," Black said, and he was back in bed with the Nurse with the Curse. Joylin was still in the bathroom and the Girl with Nine Lives was on the balcony. At least that was what Black believed. She had in fact grown bored and decided to descend in the manner to which she had become addicted.

"I am sorry," Black said to the Nurse with the Curse.

"This has never happened to me before."

"Are you sure?" the Nurse asked, less than sympathetic.

"Of course," Black said, "but in my defence I am rather tired; it has been a long... number of days and as you might have noticed I have taken something of a kicking."

"I understand all that," the Nurse said, "but it has never happened to *me* before." She sat up and gestured down her body. "*This* does not usually lead to *that*." She pointed at Black's equipment failure. Black looked at it as well.

"I am not surprised," he said, looking at his bruised abdomen. His testicles felt swollen and hard. "Don't take this as a personal slight. You just caught me on a bad day." He shifted himself round on the bed so that he was sitting up leaning against the pillows and pulled the covers over his errant genitalia.

"*You* have had a bad day," the Nurse with the Curse said, shifting to sit beside him and pulling the cover up to her waist. "I did not exactly have a great day either, and this wasn't how I thought it would end. I was looking forward to a bit of a—"

At that moment the door crashed open and Doctor Klown burst in. He stared at the bare breasts of the Nurse with the Curse in horror and shock.

"Bloody hell, McCarthy," he said, "you appear to be in bed with my wife."

"Your wife?" Black asked, looking at the Nurse with the Curse with alarm. "I had no idea."

"Doctor Klown," the Nurse said, "we are not married and quite frankly who I fuck is none of your business." She pulled the covers up over her breasts, and the doctor jerked his crimson face up in amazement and stared at her face.

"Nurse..." he said. "I am sorry... I... that is... I..."

"Yes, Doctor?"

"I... I... I... of course." He turned and left the room, closing the door behind him.

"Do you think you could lock the door," the Nurse with the Curse said to Black, "in case he decides to come back?"

"Of course," Black said. He slipped out of the bed and started to walk towards the door, and found himself in an elevator with the Girl with Nine Lives, who was laughing at his attempts not to look at her body and resultant discomfort once he had.

"Oh, really, Mr McCarthy," she said, "I really don't mind.

It is quite flattering in a way." She glanced at his erect penis. "And quite a compliment, I suppose, although…"

"Yes?" Black said, avoiding her gaze.

"Do you think you could, you know, deflate it before we leave the elevator?"

"I am trying not to think about it."

"Would you like me to…" — she reached a hand towards it — "you know… help?

"NO!" Black exclaimed, jolting away from her grasp. "That might make it worse. We can't have long."

"You are right," the Girl with Nine Lives said. "Try to think of something neutral. A distraction. I am worried it might cause more offence if we leave the elevator with you… erect. You know how people are."

"You think two naked people emerging from an elevator won't be bizarre enough."

"Not in Interfold," she said. "There are several sports clubs that promote just this sort of thing. They say it is healthy and harks back to ancient Greece."

"So we should be OK, then."

"Not exactly. Although the nudism is tolerated, public scenes of a sexual nature are prohibited."

"A sexual nature?"

"Yes." She gestured to her striped pubic hair and said, "It seems that a bit of badger is nothing to worry about but the sight of a stiffy is beyond the pale!"

"It is always the same," Black said; "the poor old penis feels the blade of the censor's knife… aha. There we are." He pointed to his rapidly declining erection. "Seems the thought of a blade was all it took. Now keep me distracted until we get into my room."

"How am I to do that?"

"I don't know. Tell me something about yourself."

"I'd rather not. Why don't you remind me about that chap you are looking for?"

"Eugenides?"

"Yes. That is the one. Any luck? Have you found him?"

"Not yet, but I am told he is still here in Interfold. I just need to track him down."

"I see."

"You did say you would help if you could."

"Yes, I did," she said. "I am not sure if it will help, but there is a someone, who unfortunately I know far too well, who has the knack of knowing who everyone in Interfold is and where they are. Don't ask me how because I don't know. I have no idea whether they will help you, but it would be worth you at least speaking to them."

"Who are they," Black said, "and where do I find them?"

"I'll write it down for you when we get to your room." She watched the elevator display as it ceased moving and the doors began to open. Black stuck his head out and, seeing only an empty corridor, turned back to tell the Girl with Nine Lives the coast was clear and was no longer in the elevator but bound to a chair in the blank white room in which he had been held captive by Dixon.

Dixon was attempting to rape Joylin. She was lying prone on the floor, semi-conscious, as Dixon ripped off her underwear. His trousers were round his ankles and Black could see sweat glistening on his hairy white behind as he threw Joylin's legs apart and lowered himself. Seeming to want her to be aware of his actions, he slapped her across the face and, taking her arm by the wrist, pushed her right hand onto his prick and grunted:

"Guide it in or I'll kill you."

Joylin appeared to comply with his order. She twisted and gripped his prick as instructed. Her left hand going up to her head as if to shield her eyes.

"Watch me, girl. You keep watching me," Dixon ordered, and he slapped her again. Joylin groaned as snot and blood spluttered from her nose. Her left hand moved behind her head as Dixon started to thrust forward as if fucking Joylin's hand. Joylin gripped him hard and vicious. Tugged his prick violently to one side with her right hand as she pulled a long silver hairpin from her hair with her left and in one smooth motion swept this down and perfectly skewered his testicles with it.

She threw him off and he collapsed to one side, making a primeval animal sound that Black could barely believe was coming from a human being. Joylin staggered to her feet, pushing her skirt down. She had red marks all over her face from the many blows Dixon had landed. One eye was swollen and blood was flowing freely from her nose and making snotty bubbles as she sucked in deep breaths. She stood over Dixon and stamped on his throat, which added a gurgling element to the animal noise. Picking up a switchblade that had fallen from Dixon's pocket, she staggered across to Black and removed the bandana that was gagging his mouth; cut through the gaffer tape that had bound his arms and legs to the chair.

"Are you OK?" Black asked, coughing and rasping.

"More or less," Joylin said. "You?"

"Yep. Nothing serious. Where is his gun?"

"Over there." Joylin pointed to the floor a few feet from where the coiled Dixon moaned. Black walked across and picked up the gun. He stood over Dixon with it held loosely at his side.

"Black?" Joylin said, and the sound of her voice seemed to resolve whatever question was in his mind. He raised the gun and shot Dixon in the head twice in quick succession.

Black left Joylin in his bathroom and went back into the main room of the suite, where the Girl with Nine Lives was. He had gone into the bathroom to get her a robe but, having been surprised to find Joylin there, had completely forgotten about it. It did not matter. The Girl with Nine Lives was wearing one of his shirts and looking pretty good in it.

"I don't know about you, but I could use a drink," she said.

"Of course," Black said; "there is a meagrely stocked, stupendously priced mini-bar over here." He walked across the room and opened the mini-bar fridge. "What can I get you? We have Trotsky vodka — a new one on me — or Pirate Gin? No mixers, though, so you might be better off with the vodka."

"Vodka is fine. Trotsky is a tolerable brand once you get used to the resemblance to paint thinners."

"It is rather warm," Black warned her. "The fridge doesn't work."

"That's OK."

"I have complained. It is as if they think simply painting it pink on the inside will keep things cold." He handed a mini bottle of Trotsky to the Girl with Nine Lives and kept one for himself.

"Vive la revolution!" the Girl with Nine Lives said, raising her bottle in a toast.

"Vive la revolution!" Black agreed, and he emptied his bottle down his throat. "Whoa! That is rough," he said with a grimace.

"I did warn you."

"Maybe a second will mask the taste of the first."

"If you have it, I will drink it."

As Black turned back to the fridge there was a knock at the door. Black looked at the Girl with Nine Lives, eyebrows raised in question.

"I'd rather no one knew I was here," she said. "I'll hop out on to the balcony just to be on the safe side."

"OK. I'll get rid of whoever it is."

"I'll take the Trotsky, though."

"What?" Black asked. "Oh, of course. Sorry." He handed the Girl with Nine Lives a second bottle of Trotsky. Waited a moment for her to hop to the balcony.

"You might want to cover up before you open the door," she suggested before hopping out of sight, closing the door behind her.

Whoever was outside the door knocked again as Black ducked quickly into the bathroom to grab a towel.

"Back already?" Joylin asked. She was wearing the only bathrobe that the suite contained. Like all Interfold bathrobes it was pink, but on Joylin it was a reasonable fit.

"There is someone at the door. Hand me that towel," Black said.

"Really?" Joylin asked, handing him a pink towel. "Do you know who it is?"

"Not yet. I was planning to cover up before opening the door."

"You could have just looked through the spy hole."

"It's broken."

"I should have guessed."

"Yep." He wrapped the towel around his waist. "Stay in here. Just in case," he said, and before she could protest he hurried back into the suite.

He opened the door to Suite 9762 to find the Nurse with the Curse standing in the corridor wearing a short red halter-neck shift dress and high-heeled shoes that looked far too big and clunky for her. The immediate impression Black had was of someone who had been in the dressing-up box or a kid wearing her mother's shoes. She pushed past him into the suite, swinging a paper bag that contained take-out. Indian by the smell that wafted out of it. Something confirmed by the logo on the bag, which read "Lal Jomi Pavilion", the name of that famous Bristol restaurant whose only other branch just happened to be in INTERFOLD — The Time Travel ~~Hotel~~ Republic.

"Since you did not arrive for our lunch date," she said, "I

thought I would forgive you and bring you dinner."

"That is very kind of you," Black said, not having to work very hard to see where this was going. "Is that wine?" He pointed at the unlabelled bottle she was holding.

"Yes, it is," she said. "I make it myself. I think this one is beetroot and horseradish. I forgot to label it. I generally use whatever I can get hold of depending on where and when we are. The tariffs on wine are stupid in Interfold, so everyone makes their own." She set the food and wine down and turned to face Black, with her legs as straight as she could get them and her hands on her hips. She eyed him up and down. "Nice outfit," she said.

Black looked back. Her hair was long, loose and dark. Just the way he liked it. The red dress was sheer and almost translucent. He could just about see the dark of her nipples pressing against the thin fabric. She was clearly not wearing a bra and he had a hunch she was not wearing anything under the dress at all. He liked what he saw and somewhere in his brain an electrical impulse moved from 0 to 1 and started to pump blood down to where it might be required, causing his erection to do what erections do and rise to the occasion. This made the towel around his waist present a quick impression of a pink tent being raised before parting like curtains and falling from his waist to the floor.

"Ah ha," she said in mock surprise, "is that for me?"

Before Black could reply she slipped the strap of the dress from her neck and shimmied it to the floor, stepped out of her shoes and moved close to Black so that her breasts were pressed against his chest. She slipped a hand around his penis, making him gasp.

"Blimey," he said, "your hands are freezing."

"Are they?" She kissed him. "Is that a bad thing?" She slipped her other hand around his balls and gave them a small squeeze.

"Gggarrrghhh," Black said, experiencing a weird combination of pleasure, pain and dizziness. His knees buckled. She squeezed harder and leant her weight against him, causing him to fall back on to the bed. "Pfffffwhhhooooooooaa," he half-said, half-exhaled as white stars flickered across his vision.

The Nurse with the Curse climbed on top of Black and straddled him. She placed one hand on his chest to steady herself, gripped his erection tight, guiding it towards her with the other hand, arched over him with her head down and long dark hair cascading to brush his skin. Had Black realised she was guiding his penis towards her lethal third orifice he would have been more alarmed than he was — although in his defence he was pretty alarmed in any case — but some unknowable instinct mixed with pain and a splash of nausea saved his life via a just-in-time delivery of the aforementioned equipment failure.

He stared at the ceiling. He stared to the left. He stared to the right. He craned his neck down and stared at her breasts. He stared at the rest of her, still feeling a little woozy, his testicles throbbing as if they had drawn down all the blood from their trouser companion in a fit of pique. *How come you get all the action*, they seemed to yell, a*nd we take all the kickings?*

The Nurse with the Curse jerked Black's limp member roughly, pulling his foreskin up over the head and quickly back down to the base. This had no effect at all. She sighed with frustration, slid down his body, took the malfunctioning tool in her mouth and ran her tongue over it, sliding it in under the foreskin in a swirling motion that had been known to bring better men than Black McCarthy to their knees. All Black wanted to do was sleep, but, as he was at this point in the narrative — technically speaking — already asleep, that was not an option.

"I am very sorry," he said as the Nurse with the Curse realised she was on to a loser and lifted her head to look at Black, with her mouth remaining connected to his ever-receding penis by a lengthy goober of saliva. She wiped her mouth with the back of her hand and flicked the goober onto his stomach with a small splash. "This has never happened to me before."

"Are you sure?" the Nurse asked in a voice that conveyed that she was less than sympathetic.

"Of course," Black said, "but in my defence I am rather tired; it has been a long... number of days and as you might have noticed I have taken something of a kicking."

"I understand all that," the Nurse said, "but it has never happened to me before." She sat up and gestured down her body. "This does not usually lead to that." She pointed at Black's equipment failure. Black looked at it as well.

"I am not surprised," he said, looking at his bruised abdomen. His testicles felt swollen and hard. "Don't take

this as a personal slight. You just caught me on a bad day."
He shifted himself round on the bed so that he was sitting
up leaning against the pillows and found himself, like Joylin,
in the bathroom. Why was she always in his bathroom?

And why was he back in that bloody sauna? Bathroom.
Sauna. Bathroom. Sauna. And why was Joylin in the sauna?
That was wrong. Joylin had not been in the sauna. Had she?
But she was in the sauna now, wearing the pink INTERFOLD
bathrobe and beside him in the corner reading a book. The
Girl with Nine Lives was in the sauna as well, and the Nurse
with the Curse. They were both naked, the same as Black.
They were sitting across the room on the highest platform,
talking quietly to each other, and Black could only just hear
them. They were speaking in a language he had never heard
before. Maybe Magyar or Finnish. He couldn't catch a single
word that had a familiar sound.

"What are they saying?" he asked Joylin.

"I have no idea," Joylin replied.

"You don't sound very interested."

"I am not."

"Why not? It might be important."

"How so?"

"They are both Interfold residents with potential
information."

"And I am trying to read this book but you are interrupting
me."

"I am sorry, Joylin. You carry on." He kept quiet for a
moment, watching her reading. She turned a page.

"What are you reading?"

"Oh, for goodness' sake, McCarthy, you are like a child!"

"Sorry."

"I am reading *The Waste Land* by T.S. Eliot." She returned
to the book. He watched her for a moment, and then turned
his attention back to the Girl with Nine Lives and the Nurse
with the Curse and noticed for the first time that both had
the distinctive badger-like stripes that have featured several
times now in the narrative of this book.

He watched as the unintelligible exchange appeared to
grow more heated. The Nurse with the Curse was gesturing
like a hungry Italian in an attempt to emphasise a point.
Every time she raised her arms her breasts wobbled a little.
Black watched, mesmerised.

"Joylin?" he said.

Joylin turned to see Black McCarthy sitting beside her with a fully extended erection. "That is the bloody limit, McCarthy," she said, and she stormed out of the sauna, slamming the door behind her.

Black stood up in protest. "But Joylin..." he started to say, and then he felt a hand on his shoulder and turned round. The Girl with Nine Lives was right there, close in his personal space, balancing on her one leg.

"Would you like me to..." — she reached a hand towards his erection — "you know... help?

"I could help too," the Nurse with the Curse said, standing shoulder to shoulder with the Girl with Nine Lives and reaching out a hand.

Both hands, both freezing despite their being in a sauna, connected with Black's penis at the same moment and he immediately erupted in a semi-conscious spasm that rippled out of his dreaming brain into physical reality as he ejaculated, and ejaculated and ejaculated.

It felt like it wouldn't stop. It was like a fire hose. It was like his body was emptying itself of a backlog. Pumping and pumping and pumping. An electric quiver of panic kicked up from his balls to his brain and back again. He tensed, rigid, arching his back as his waking brain registered the unfortunate fact in a moment of horror familiar to every teenage boy: he wasn't simply dreaming. He was actually, genuinely, physically ejaculating and he could not stop it happening.

"Bloody hell, McCarthy," Joylin said, punching him awake, "are you for real?" She was half-sitting, half-lying next to him in bed, the covers thrown back away from them both. She was wearing pink panties and a black vest which she was holding rucked up around her chest, baring the smooth, soft, perfectly light brown skin of her stomach. On the side of her stomach closest to Black a thick, slick line of semen glistened as it slid slowly down towards the sheets.

Black simply stared at it in dumb horror and wished that, like the Man Who Fell Through Floors, he had the knack of disappearing at will.

CHAPTER THIRTEEN

1 The Man Who Dreamt He Was Dreaming was no longer dreaming. He was no longer asleep but lying with his eyes closed, taking long deep breaths. He opened his eyes and stared up in the half-light created by the heavy curtains drawn against the windows. He supposed he should think about getting up. His bladder agreed. By any humanoid standard it had held out for an inordinate length of time, but enough was enough. He rolled over, swung his legs out of the bed and tried to sit up but instead fell out onto the floor as his weak limbs protested at this sudden call to action. Progress was progress, though, he thought, and at least he was now lying face-down on the floor rather than on his back in bed.

He pushed himself up onto all fours and crawled to the bathroom before pulling himself upright using the sink for support. He looked at his baggy eyes in the mirror and blew out a foul-smelling sigh.

"Sweet Jesus!" He reached for the mouthwash.

Urinating proved difficult. He tried standing, as would be normal, but he kept swaying and pissing on his feet, so he sat down like a girl. Then he couldn't go. Sat there like an idiot concentrating without success before kneeling before the toilet with his dick hanging over the rim and resting his forehead on the edge of the half-lowered toilet seat.

After that he cleaned his teeth, washed his face twelve times with ice-cold water from the tap marked "hot", and as his legs got used to the evolutionary concept of an upright ape, he pulled on some sweatpants and a T-shirt and went into the kitchen to make coffee.

As he sat on his favourite leather chair a short while later, drinking treacle-thick espresso and munching on crackers slathered with Marmite, he felt a cool breeze blowing in through the open window. It did not cross his mind that the window being open was odd. He assumed he had forgotten to close it before he fell asleep, whenever that was, is or at some point will be. Either that or his clearly absent and most likely now ex-girlfriend the Girl with Nine Lives had left it open on her way out.

He thought about getting up and closing it, but before he could make a decision he felt a sharp prick in the left side of his neck like a particularly vicious insect bite. He moved his right hand up to feel the site of the sting, but it only got halfway before falling limp into his lap. He couldn't move it. It sat limp and dead, palm up. He tried to move the other arm, but this was dead as well. He tried to turn his neck to look over his shoulder but found that he could not move at all. He was paralysed and immobile. Was he still asleep after all? Was this some weird sleep-induced paralysis? He was sure he was awake this time. It felt different. More senses were in play. He could smell the coffee. That meant he was awake. He was sure of it. Maybe this was just a delayed repercussion of the weeks asleep.

"Keep calm," he tried to say, but instead dribbled something unintelligible.

The Bag Lady/Assassin walked slowly around in front of the Man Who Dreamt He Was Dreaming so that he could understand the reason for his paralysis. She was holding a Martian nerve gun. Of course he had no idea what it was she was holding, but it was clear she was responsible for his sudden paralysis.

"Immobiliser serum," she said with a small shrug of the

shoulders, and she smacked him hard on the bridge of the nose with the handle of the gun. His nose exploded as it broke in a splatter of bloody mucus and a strangled exclamation gargled from his throat. The pain was unreal. He felt like he had been hit in the face with something hard and metal, which may be stating the obvious, but you try being hit in the face by a gun having been given a Martian immobilising serum that removes your instinctive ability to try to avoid the blow.

She stood over him. Her long dark hair was tied back. She was wearing a cropped black sports vest and Lycra shorts that she had borrowed/stolen from the Girl with the Broken Neck. She looked him over. Yes. This was the right one. She was sure this time. No more mistakes. She walked out of his field of vision. He heard a clattering from the kitchen and a short while later she returned holding two kitchen knives. One with a short, sharp blade that he used for peeling fruit. The other a long, smooth-bladed carving knife. Both good-quality chef-grade instruments. She put both knives on the coffee table in front of the Man Who Dreamt He Was Dreaming. She stood looking at him for a few terrible minutes, hands on hips, and then disappeared again.

She returned with some scissors and began to cut his clothing off, pulled his legs forward to remove his sweatpants and continued cutting until he was flopped back naked in the chair. She reached for the knives.

She worked with the detailed eye and knowledge of an expert intent on taking him over thresholds of pain that he had no idea existed. Every time it overwhelmed him she would pause just long enough for it to stabilise and then she would set to work again.

Martian immobilising serum is nasty stuff. Not only does it immobilise the victim whilst leaving all sensation intact, but it has a devious side effect that switches off the human body's natural ability to project temporarily pain-dulling chemicals to wound sites. In addition, it has an amplifying effect so that any pain inflicted is signalled to the brain at roughly five times human normal. The Bag Lady/Assassin found that this made her job all the more enjoyable and it greatly expanded the field of sensation in which she could work.

She paused as the noise emitted by the Man Who Dreamt He Was Dreaming reached a tell-tale high pitch, and smiled as she waited for it to subside. It was good to be back at work.

2 The Dwarf with the Horse, Pedro and their ever-present escort of ASSIIR agents remained in the Red Light Basement. The agents had a duty to execute and could not step down until they had succeeded. This had proved harder than they had anticipated and many attempts at escorting Pedro and the Dwarf out of the south-west exit — which was accessed via the emergency exit from the Red Light Basement — had all proven unsuccessful.

Every time they had been escorted out of the door through which Black McCarthy and the Man Who Fell Through Floors had thrown the Bag Lady Who Was Thrown Away, the Dwarf with the Horse and Pedro had immediately reappeared through the main door of the Red Light Basement. They tried it seven times with one of the three agents going first to see what happened. Each time the agents just found themselves out in the service yard with the garbage, yet when they sent Pedro and the Dwarf out they reappeared again in a doorway on the opposite side of the bar as if both doors stood across the same threshold. On the final attempt the agents spaced themselves out so that Agent No. 3 could see the backs of Pedro and the Dwarf through the emergency exit, Agent No. 2 occupied the door from the bar to the corridor that led to the exit, and Agent No. 1 manned the main entrance.

"Exiting now," Agent No. 3 called to Agent No. 2.

"Exiting now," Agent No. 2 called to Agent No. 1.

"Entering now," Agent No. 1 called to Agent No. 2.

"Entering now," Agent No. 2 called to Agent No. 3.

"I can still see them here," Agent No. 3 called to Agent No. 2.

"He says can still see them," Agent No. 2 called to Agent No. 1.

"That's impossible," Agent No. 1 called back.

Agent No. 2 moved to position himself where he could see the main entrance and see down the corridor. From this position he could see the front of the Dwarf with the Horse and Pedro entering from one door as their backs remained visible in the other.

"I can see them twice," he called to his compadres. "I can see them twice."

After that they abandoned the attempts and left Pedro and the Dwarf alone at the bar while they sat in glum silence near the emergency exit.

"Look at those dummies," Pedro said. "Barely enough

brain cells to keep one head warm, never mind three!"

"Yep," the Dwarf said.

"Dumb, Dumber and Dumbest."

"Yep," the Dwarf said.

Pedro chuckled. "I don't think they have the faintest idea how stupid they are."

"Yep," the Dwarf said.

"Is that all you have got to say on the matter?" Pedro asked, still smiling his big horsey smile.

"Yep," the Dwarf said.

"Dumbasses," Pedro said.

"I get the point, Pedro. Give it a rest."

"OK, buddy. Keep your shades on," Pedro said, but he continued to chuckle.

"Go on," the Dwarf said, "say it one more time and then let it go, OK?"

"If they were so intent on getting us out of here," Pedro said, "why did they let McCarthy bring us back? I mean, we were already out of this place, it would have been easy, but I don't think it occurred to a single one of them. Can you believe it?"

"Yes, Pedro, I can," the Dwarf said. "I was there. It happened. We got away with it. So far."

"What do you mean, 'so far'?"

"Do you think they are going to let it go?"

"Why not? We did what they asked."

"Yeah, but it didn't work, did it? We are still here."

"So?"

"So they are going to try something else and keep trying until they get rid of us," the Dwarf said.

"Relax, buddy, they haven't got any idea what to try next."

"What if they call that woman?"

"That woman?"

"Yeah, that woman," the Dwarf said. "The one who called you a well-hung cheval sandwich."

"Don't remind me!" Pedro shivered.

"She seemed pretty mean."

"Brrrrrr." Pedro shook himself. "Reminded me of that girl from..."

"Yeah?"

"Yeah, you know... the one from..."

"Does she really remind you of another girl?"

"Yeah, yeah, of course she does; I just can't seem to put a hoof on which one. There have been so many." Pedro shook his head, thinking.

"There sure have been a few," the Dwarf said, and they both lapsed into silence, thinking of one girl or another from this place or that time.

The three ASSIIR agents were disagreeing about the next move.

"I say we try again," Agent No. 2 proposed.

"That is a waste of time," Agent No. 1 said, folding his arms.

"I need a shower," Agent No. 3 said, not listening to the other two and looking at a door that was marked "ARTISTS ONLY". "Do you think they have a shower in there? I am going to check it out." He walked through the door, leaving his companions to continue their disagreement.

The Dwarf with the Horse and Pedro watched in silence as the two ASSIIR agents approached.

"What do you think we should do next?" Agent No. 1 asked Pedro.

"What are you asking him for?" the Dwarf asked.

"Because we deduce that he is the one with the brains," Agent No. 2 said.

"Bloody typical," the Dwarf said. "Pick on the little guy. You regulars are all the same."

"Well, all right then," Agent No. 1 said; "what do you suggest we do now?"

"I am quite happy where I am."

"That is not particularly helpful," Agent No. 1 said.

"And not really an option," Agent No. 2 added.

"If we simply wait here, someone will eventually be sent to check that we have escorted you from Interfold via the south-west exit as instructed," Agent No. 1 said.

"Which will end badly for all of us," Agent No. 2 said.

"So what do you two suggest?" Pedro asked.

"My colleague here thinks we should come clean and inform the councillor that despite our best efforts we have been unable to execute her instructions and request new ones," Agent No. 2 said.

"But he disagrees and thinks we should just continue repeating our attempts until someone from the agency arrives to check on us, at which point we make it their problem since we will be witnessed in the active pursuit of our duty," Agent No. 1 said.

"Interesting," Pedro said. He considered both proposals. "I favour plan B myself."

"Typical," said Agent No. 1.

"It is very simple," Pedro said. "If you return to the councillor you will be dropping us in it. We will then seek to improve our situation by pointing out that we did indeed leave Interfold territory but that you — er — three" — he looked around for the third agent — "brought us back."

"What?" Agent No. 1 asked.

"Oh," Agent No. 2 said, "good point, good point. So you agree my idea is indeed the best course of action."

"I do," Pedro said.

"There you go," Agent No. 2 said to Agent No. 1.

"How is that different from my proposal just to stay here and lie low?" the Dwarf asked.

"It isn't really," Pedro said, "except that we need to make a show of at least being willing to be ejected from Interfold from time to time for the sake of good order and all that."

"For the sake of good order, eh, Pedro?"

"Yes. For the sake of good order."

"Now *you* are reminding me of a girl."

"Oh, yes?" Pedro said. "Which one?"

3 There were times when the neglected and erratically maintained infrastructure of INTERFOLD — The Time Travel ~~Hotel~~ Republic had its advantages. The plumbing, for instance, was ill-supplied. Water was not guaranteed to be available on all levels at all times, and it was often pure chance whether any of this water would emerge from a tap in tune with its designation. Some of the plumbing had been completed by a French subcontractor who had connected the hot supply to taps marked C regardless of the fact that the remainder were marked H. Others had been connected by off-world subcontractors who had no knowledge of the Roman alphabet and simply made it all up as they went along.

This wayward approach saved the life of the Man Who Lived in a Vacuum Cleaner. He had thought his number was once more up as he was dragged down into the U-bend of the toilet in Alex from Mars's bathroom, but he was shot in a torrent into a wider sewer pipe that was far from full and flowing slowly as it had been installed at too shallow an angle. He thus found himself washed along with his head above water in a slowly descending spiral through the levels of Interfold. Had he been familiar with the concept of water parks he might have noticed a similarity. As his terror subsided he found he could sit up as he was swept along, not unlike a kid in a corkscrew tube. A tube made of translucent plastic through which dull red light filtered from time to time. A tube that, yes, smelled pretty much as you would expect it would, but that he could live with if he had to.

The ride went on and on and on. He grew bored. Alternated sitting up and lying back. In one particularly shallow and slow-moving section he even played with the surprisingly large penis for a bit to relieve the tedium. A few floors lower the water started to speed along and so he sang himself a chorus or two of *Yes, We Have No Bananas* to keep his spirits up.

Eventually, after an indeterminate period of time, instantaneously or at some point in time yet to be determined but most certainly in the future (reminders and alarm calls are available from reception), the Man Who Lived in a Vacuum Cleaner reached the end of the tube. He slid majestically from the pipe, sitting up and peering into the darkness as he went over the edge and felt himself falling. Limbs flailing he smacked into a body of cold water some feet below and went under.

He rose spluttering, gagging and choking, his nose, eyes and ears full of putrescence. He rubbed his eyes clear and trod water. The water was lapping against him in small waves making him bob up and down. He let the water take him, trying to feel if there was a current that would sweep him along if only he kept his head up and his mind awake. In some murky indeterminate distance he could see a faint red light. In the absence of any other options heading towards it seemed the only plan worth consideration, so he adopted it and struck out in the general direction of the beacon. Stopping from time to time to check he was on the right course, he thrashed along, making less progress than he had hoped. As a city boy from the 1920s life had not afforded him many opportunities for swimming.

As he paused for breath and to check his bearings he saw a silhouette of something large and dark floating ahead. Perhaps a log or piece of garbage that he could use as a raft or at the very least an aid to buoyancy. He swam towards it and tried to climb aboard. It was twice his height in length and shaped a little like a cigar. As he tried to climb on to it his hands sank into the soft brown surface. The stench was awful and seemed to wash up his nose and envelop his senses. His eyes sang and he was deaf from the shock of the smell. Trying hard not to vomit he pushed himself on, clawing his way on to the top of his lifeboat.

He lay flat so as not to cause the turd to roll over and deposit him back in the water. His face, hands, arms, body smothered and smeared in the stink. He didn't care. If this was his only hope of not drowning he would take it. Chance is chance, and so far he had found that things tended to work out in the end as long as you hung on and did not give up. He just hoped, as the smell enveloped him and the excrement painted all over his body started to dry, that he would not have to wait too long for the next break to present itself.

4 Black McCarthy stood in a corridor looking at the napkin on which the Girl with Nine Lives had written the apartment address of the person she had suggested might be able to assist him. He checked the number again against the doors and walked on, checking door numbers as he went.

He had almost forgotten about the note that morning until, on lifting up a carton of left-over aloo-gobi which he had decided would make an adequate breakfast, he had found the napkin. This had given him an objective for the day and also a useful subject changer to utilise in breaking the embarrassed silence that had gripped him since waking.

"I had forgotten about this," he said to Joylin.

"What is it?" she asked, emerging from the bathroom dressed ready for work on reception.

He explained.

"What about the Dragon Lady?"

"I am meant to report back via Dixon."

"Oh."

"I feel that I have given him my full report and have nothing to add. So I am going to work on the assumption that she will come looking for me at some point and I will worry about it when she does."

Joylin nodded agreement without smiling.

"How do I look?" she asked. "I have to return to work. My absence might arouse suspicion."

"You look OK," Black said, walking up to her and looking into her eyes. "You have covered the bruises quite well. It is only up close that you can see them."

"Good."

"I'll follow this up and check in on you later."

She had left and he had set off to find the thirteenth-floor apartment that the Girl with Nine Lives had written on the napkin. Having found the particular elevator that permitted access to the thirteenth floor, he explored the labyrinthine corridors past numbered apartments that steadily ascended to the one he was seeking. He knocked loudly on the door and waited. Nothing. He knocked again. Again nothing. He put an ear to the door and listened. He was sure he could hear something. The door opened and a girl with long dark hair, tied back, looked round the door at him.

"Oh," she said, "it's you." She stared at him, her face blank but her mind calculating. "Come in." She stood back, holding the door open, and gestured for Black to enter.

Bemused at being expected, Black walked into the apartment wondering if this was going to be easier than he had thought. She closed the door and followed him. The Martian nerve gun was heavy in her hand as, holding it by the muzzle, she swung it like an axe at the back of Black's head.

The glancing blow knocked Black sideways into the wall and his knees buckled, but he was only stunned and not out cold as she pounced on him, pulling his head back and kneeing him viciously in the spine. Before he could do anything about it he was face-down on the carpet with his hands cable-gripped behind his back. She dragged him into the main room of the apartment by the collar and pulled him up into a kneeling position before cable-gripping his ankles as well to stop him from trying to stand up.

Black stared at her as she stood over him with a large

unearthly pistol hanging in her left hand. She stared back and stepped aside so that he could see the bloody mess that had once been the Man Who Dreamt He Was Dreaming. Many of us would have been undone by such a sight, but Black had seen worse and in any case had never been much of a puker. His stomach, as had too often been the case, was stronger than his instinct for danger.

"I think you have me confused for someone else," he said to the Bag Lady/Assassin. "I simply came here looking for some information. I assume from whoever that is." He nodded at the steaming mess on the sofa. "This is none of my business and I can assure you I want no connection with it, so why not just let me go?"

The Bag Lady/Assassin stared at him. It was an obvious deception, but she had beaten him to the finish and that was that. It was her own fault that a second assassin had been hired to finish the job. She would just have to deal with the inconvenience.

"It is not your fault," she said; "I should have finished the job sooner. She should have been more patient, though. There was no need to send you."

"What?" Black asked, not understanding.

"I cannot just let you go." She raised the gun. She would immobilise him, unbind him and leave him here in the apartment with the knives in his hands. She clicked the nerve gun onto a low setting. Enough to give her an hour to get clear, at which point she would alert the authorities.

"But you don't understand," Black said. "This is all a mistake. I am looking for a man called Eugenides, that is all. I have no idea what this is all about; my client is not a woman of any species."

"Liar." She raised the gun, holding it in both hands and squinting with one eye closed as she aimed carefully for his neck, but before she could squeeze the trigger the Man Who Fell Through Floors crashed through the ceiling, smashed into her and knocked her down. The gun skittered away across the floor. He jumped up and ran after it before the Bag Lady/ Assassin could recover. He scooped the strange gun from the floor and in one swift motion turned and fired. The micro-dart hit her in the stomach and quivered in her pale midriff as she lay on the floor twitching. She tried to lift a hand to the vibrating needle as it disappeared through her skin. In a second the serum had done its work. She flopped back immobilised, her eyes glaring angrily at the Man Who Fell Through Floors.

"I have to say, buddy," Black said, "your timing is impeccable. How did you know where I was?"

"Joylin," the Man Who Fell Through Floors said. "I needed to see you and she said this was where you were. The rest was just luck. Come on, we need to get out of here."

"For sure," Black said, "but I am somewhat restrained."

"Oh, of course." He retrieved the scissors the Bag Lady/Assassin had used earlier and cut Black free. Black put a hand to the back of his head. Stared at the fingers that came back wet with blood.

"What did you need me for?"

"To tell you that Interfold executed one of its sneaky silent relocations in the night."

"I had no idea."

"Of course not. That is the intention."

"So where are we now?"

"We are in the city of Bath."

"Bath? But isn't that...?"

"Yes, it is. Ask me when we are."

"When we are?"

"Yes, when we are."

"When are we?"

"We have arrived in Bath on the very day that I fell though my first floor and wound up in Interfold."

"You are kidding."

"I am not."

"So what are you waiting for? You need to get out of here."

"Yes, yes, I know. But there is no point being too early or there will be two of me in the same time and place, and I have no idea what the ramifications of that are, so I need to time my arrival to match my exit, if you see what I mean, otherwise—"

"I see the problem," Black said, not entirely understanding but not wanting to let it show. "So what happens now?"

"We should get out of here, for a start."

"Good point." Black started for the door.

"No, not that way," the Man Who Fell Through Floors said; "too slow. Come here."

Black approached cautiously and stood next to him.

"Not like that." He turned and hugged Black and BANG

they were off, riffling through the floors at an incredible speed. Black barely had time to comprehend the motion of layers of building whipping by when they ripped through the final floor and thus through the ceiling of the reception hall of INTERFOLD — The Time Travel ~~Hotel~~ Republic.

"Roll when we hit," the Man Who Fell Through Floors said as they decelerated sharply. Black did as he was bid and rolled like a parachutist on impact. Arms crossed across his chest and knees up, he rolled over and then spun across the polished marble floor out of control. He thumped into the reception station and stood up, brushing himself down.

"What happened this time?" Joylin asked, staring at the blood on his neck and collar.

"The usual, Joylin, the usual."

"Come on," the Man Who Fell Through Floors shouted as he leapt up and ran towards the door. "Did you feel that?"

"Feel what?" Black asked.

"What is going on?" Joylin asked.

"A tremor," the Man Who Fell Through Floors said.

"A tremor?" Black asked.

"Yes, a tremor."

"Do you mean a pre-relocation tremor?" Joylin said.

"Quite possibly, and that means I have to get out of here. I am not missing this opportunity."

"Go on, then," Black said, "get out of here."

"Where are you going?" Joylin asked.

"Home," the Man Who Fell Through Floors said, and he ran towards the door. An elevator pinged in the background somewhere as doors opened.

"BLACK McCARTHY," a woman's voice boomed out, "STOP RIGHT THERE."

Black and Joylin turned towards the sound of the voice. The Man Who Fell Through Floors stopped at the entrance and stared. Smoke billowed out of the elevator as the Dragon Lady and two triumvirates of ASSIIR agents emerged from the fog.

"ARREST THEM ALL," she boomed, sucking on a cigar, smoke curling from her nostrils.

"Go!" Black shouted to the Man Who Fell Through Floors.

"You go as well," Joylin said to Black. "I'll hold them off." She pulled the gun she had originally given to Black, and fired over the heads of the agents. Black grabbed her arm and pulled her towards the Man Who Fell Through Floors.

"Come on, Joylin," he said, "I think we have burned our bridges here."

"Black!" The Man Who Fell Through Floors threw something in Black's direction. "Try this." It was the Martian nerve gun. Black caught it and, dropping to one knee, fired off three micro-darts in the direction of the agents just as Joylin fired another shot over their heads and the agents dived for what little cover was available in the spacious reception hall. One ASSIIR agent fell limp, the other two darts doing little more than immobilising a couple of sofas that were otherwise engaged in keeping out of trouble.

"Come on, Joylin," Black said again, pulling her arm, and they both ran after the Man Who Fell Through Floors who had disappeared through the main doors.

Once outside they ran down the steps and into a busy street. Behind them INTERFOLD flickered and morphed into the buildings of Bath, seeming at once something separate and something wholly part of the city. Black stopped and turned back, staring at it, marvelling at how the doors and windows of the buildings of Bath were at once doors and windows of the walls of INTERFOLD and yet not of INTERFOLD. Above him the high-rises and iconic INTERFOLD chimneys shimmered.

"How does it do that?" he asked.

"This is not the time," Joylin said. "Come on." Pulling his arm she ran along the street, pushing her way through the crowd. "And in any case the correct question should be 'why does it do it?'"

"Where is Floors?"

"Up ahead. I can see him. Over there, heading for the other side of that main road."

The Man Who Fell Through Floors was on a mission. He knew exactly where he was going. He strode along the crowded pavements dodging tourists, shoppers and people gawping at the apparition of INTERFOLD – The Time Travel Hotel Republic. He reached the corner and turned left onto a street that Black noted was called Milsom Street. Black and Joylin were still on the opposite side of the road as he turned. Traffic was gridlocked between them as people stepped out of their cars and craned their necks up to look at the walls of INTERFOLD flickering where they ought not to have been.

The Wolf materialised at their sides and leapt forward,

snapping his jaws at people to clear a path, before falling back beside Black.

"What is going on, McCarthy?" he asked. "Why have you left Interfold again? Have you located Eugenides?"

"Not as such, Wolf," Black said, following Joylin as she crossed the street between stationary cars. "Let's just say the situation was no longer conducive to my staying."

"So what's the plan?"

"The plan?"

"Yes, the plan. I assume you have one?"

"I do indeed, Wolf, and the most important element is to follow that man." He pointed to the Man Who Fell Through Floors, who was zig-zagging his way down Milsom Street towards the bookstore where his INTERFOLD journey had begun, would begin and was indeed beginning at that very moment. "You could double back and check we are not being followed by any ASSIIR agents."

"Could I, McCarthy?"

"Yes, Wolf."

"Good point. I am on it, McCarthy. You can update me when you get back," and with that he did what was customary and disappeared.

Black ran to catch up with Joylin. The Man Who Fell Through Floors was only five shop fronts away from them. Black could see the windows of the bookstore on the opposite side of the road.

"Look, Joylin," he said, pointing.

"What at?"

"Over there, going into the bookstore, it's him — the other him, I mean — just as Moe described it."

"You mean Dave."

"Oh, come on, Joylin, really? Now?"

"Sorry, couldn't resist it. Is that the younger Man Who Is About to Fall Through a Floor?"

"Yes, it is."

"Kooky."

Up ahead the Man Who Fell Through Floors was waving and shouting.

"Melissa. Melissa. I'm here, I'm here."

Black and Joylin watched as a red-haired woman wearing a black suede jacket and a white shirt turned and looked in the general direction of the Man Who Fell Through Floors, trying to locate the source of his voice. Her eyes found the husband she had only moments before seen walk into the bookstore behind her, now away from her on the other side of the street. He was wearing different clothes, had different hair, looked several kilos thinner and appeared several years older. Confused, she turned back and looked at the bookstore.

"Melissa," he called again and her head switched back to him. She looked dazed, confused, unfocused. She stepped forward towards him and stumbled as her foot slipped on a loose kerb stone. Her ankle twisted beneath her and she fell hard into the street and straight into the path of a large black BMW whose owner had chosen that moment to accelerate forward into a free parking space. She was almost horizontal when the car hit her. She was thrown against another parked car at a bizarre angle and slid over it and onto the pavement. Her head cracking back into the rough stone with a tell-tale snap.

The Man Who Fell Through Floors pushed through the rapidly collecting crowd. He fell to his knees. She was dead. He held her limp hand as, shaking, incoherent and unbelieving as he was, the floor for once refused to swallow him up.

Black and Joylin pushed through the crowd, trying to reach him.

"Coming through, coming through," Black said. "This lady is a doctor; let us through, please." They reached the Man Who Fell Through Floors, who looked up at them, pleading.

"What am I going to do?" he said.

Black stared at the Man Who Fell Through Floors. Joylin stared at Black. He knew this was the moment when he would have to be the one with the answer for a change. The moment when he rather than Joylin, the Man Who Fell Through Floors, the Wolf, fate, blind luck or divine intervention would determine the next move. He stared at them both without a clue for a long stupid pregnant pause as the reality of the situation sank in.

"You have to go back," he said.

"But Black..." Joylin said.

"I know. I know. Not that way. Interfold could relocate before we get there."

"Then how?" the Man Who Fell Through Floors asked.

"The same way you got there in the first place," Black said. "Come on; we haven't got long." He put his hand down to the Man Who Fell Through Floors, pulled him up and pushed him towards the bookstore. "Help me, Joylin."

Between them they pushed the protesting Man Who Fell Through Floors through the doors of the bookstore.

"Down there," Black said, pointing down some stairs, "and quickly; he has already been down there for a few minutes."

Joylin had no idea what Black meant but led the way down the stairs, pulling one hand of the Man Who Fell Through Floors as Black pushed him from behind.

"In there," Black said, pointing through a door at the end of the stairs, "and fast."

"What is happening?" Joylin asked.

"The stairs are melting away; get through the door and grab hold of the other Man Who Fell Through Floors and don't let go of either of them."

Joylin still leading, they all rushed through the door to find the younger Man Who Fell Through Floors saying to a young man, "What's the date?"

"NOW!" Black shouted, and Joylin, the Man Who Fell Through Floors and Black McCarthy all pounced on the younger Man Who Fell Through Floors at the very moment that his own personal temporal anomaly opened up beneath his feet for the first time and all four of them disappeared into it.

The young man stood frozen and bug-eyed with a droning telephone receiver in his hand. He had no idea who it was he should call in such a situation and what he would say if he did. He considered things for a moment and then did what any of us would do in his place; he put the receiver down and poured himself a large Trotsky.

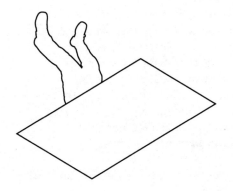

FURTHER READING

The following books were influential in the writing of Time Travel Hotel, something that I feel I should acknowledge here and encourage you to read some or all of them:

Death and the Penguin by Andrey Kurkov
The Book of Laughter and Forgetting by Milan Kundera
The Unbearable Lightness of Being by Milan Kundera
Catch 22 by Joseph Heller
The Wasteland and other poems by T.S. Eliot
Sombrero Fallout by Richard Brautigan
Slaughterhouse 5 by Kurt Vonnegut
Zazie in the Metro by Raymond Queneau
Swag, 52 Pickup, Bandits, Mr Paradise by Elmore Leonard
The Histories by Herodotus
Stasiland by Anna Funder
The Hitchhiker's Guide to the Galaxy by Douglas Adams
Europe, a History by Norman Davies
Istanbul, the Imperial City by John Freely
Dada & Surrealism by C.W.E. Bigsby
All My Friends are Superheroes by Andrew Kaufman
Cancer Party by Andrew Raymond Drennan
Morvern Callar by Alan Warner
The Adventures of Tintin by Hergé

In addition the following TV shows and films will also prove useful reference:

Hong Kong Phooey
The Simpsons
Dr Who
Monty Python's Flying Circus (the Cheese Shop sketch in particular)
Monty Python's the Meaning of Life
Star Wars (Episode 4 : A New Hope)

THANKS AND ACKNOWLEDGMENTS

Thanks are due to Kate Birnie, Philip Brocklehurst, Mark Steele-Mortimer, Howie Laurie, Anna Freeman, Mairi Campbell-Jack and Sally Jenkinson for beta reading. Sally especially for the detailed notes and suggestions. Dominic Brookman for the perfect cover design. Harriet Evans whose editing improved the text immeasurably, and in particular for writing in the margins:

"...one of the things that makes your style so readable is that you never force the reader out of the story to go running for a dictionary (this might sound like a backhanded compliment, but I swear it isn't; it's infuriating when a writer bypasses the best word for the job in favour of one that he thinks will make him look clever)"

The book is quietly dedicated to my daughter Lucy who was desperate to read it during all the long years it took to complete, but was far too young to be allowed anywhere near it. I hope when, once old enough, she does read it that by the time she reaches this page, she is not too appalled.

BONUS MATERIAL

The nature of

What is a man?

XXXXXXXXXXX

Dogs and locusts

Desperate fling

Cosmic queen

Rin Tin Tin,

Fighter jets

★★★★★★★★★

Superyachts

★★★★★★★★

★★★★

Unlucky numbers

Fairy godfathers

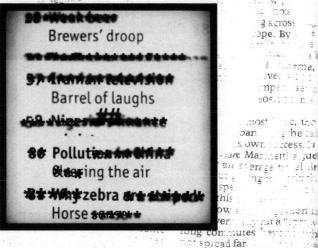

Brewers' droop

Barrel of laughs

Pollution

Clearing the air

Why zebra are striped

Horse sense

DIY chromosomes

Something new under the sun

Sexual selection

Don't cramp my style

Shovel face

o understand!

happy minds in unhealthy bo

CORPORATE CULTURE
(& HOW TO SURVIVE IT)
-A NOVEL-

1 Mr Pin Stripe was snoring like a snorting warthog. I was wide awake. There was no way I could be anything else. The noise was an immense flatulent gurgling. It roared out of his gaping mouth and battered my ears. I was travelling East above Iran on a British Airways flight destined for Singapore with Mr Pin Stripe, my boss at The Corporation, and we were en route to Cambodia. An intelligent man and experienced business traveller, Mr Pin Stripe was well respected throughout The Corporation as a dedicated and accomplished professional. Corporate Man to the core, trained and modelled to Corporate standards. As reliable in performance as any of The Corporation's world famous brands.

We were to attend a two day conference in Phnom Penh. A prospect I did not welcome. Of all the cities in East Asia to hold a conference The Corporation chose Phnom Penh. A city I feared might prove dangerous. I had visions of the entire 100 attendees being kidnapped and ransomed by Khmer Rouge bandits before the weekend. Phnom Penh. If a dangerous location was the order why not Mogadishu. Why compromise on the danger factor. My intestines twitched at the thought.

Phnom Penh was the choice of The General. He had an penchant for Phnom Penh and was not a man to be persuaded otherwise. If he had testosterone to burn in Phnom Penh then in Phnom Penh it would burn. That meant myself, Mr Pin Stripe and a troupe of our colleagues had to tag along for the sake of Corporate professionalism.

The General was CEO of The International Unit, a subdivision of the vast Corporation responsible for conquering new territory charting new and dangerous waters. It was in The International Unit that I found myself employed. I say found because I came to be on that particular British Airways flight to Singapore through a series of short sighted decisions and a general drift of misadventure. I had been leaping from short plank to short plank for 6 years and was finally questioning my lack of vision.

On the damp February morning six years earlier when I walked into the employment agency in Bristol for whom I was temping — to pick up a new assignment — I had no idea The Corporation even existed. The name meant nothing to me.

"The what?" I said to Angela the Employment Agency Executive.

"The Corporation," she replied, "one of the world's largest companies and an excellent employer. They make that toilet cleaner that's always on the telly and dog food I think."

"Oh right." I tried to look impressed. It meant nothing to me, although it sounded like an odd combination.

"It is only a temporary position but there is the possibility of it being made permanent within six months if they like you. It really is an excellent opportunity with prospects if they take you on, what do you think?"

"Sounds too good to miss. I'll take it." I didn't have much choice. I needed the money and the data processing job they had me on would have rendered me a vegetable within the week. Solid reasons for a career move.

Six years later I was sat on a plane with Mr Pin Stripe as a result of that conversation. Heading for a conference in the capital city of a country which, at the time we were travelling, the British Foreign Office officially advised British citizens to avoid. The land owning Managing Director of The Corporation's International Unit knew no fear in charting new markets, however. The General saw himself as a fearless pioneer, it would take more than the Khmer Rouge, minefields, kidnapping and the British Foreign Office to put him off a conference venue once the urge had seized him.

Back on that February morning, Angela had picked up the telephone and fixed the details with The Corporation's personnel department. I had no reason to doubt the decision and to regret it now would be pointless. If I had not taken that job a whole series of experiences and people would not have wandered into my life in. I wouldn't have written my great unpublished novel, I would not have stumbled into the Marketing Department of the International Unit, and more importantly I would not have found myself sitting on a plane en route to Phnom Penh watching the moon rise over northern Iran while Mr Pin Stripe roared beside me. The moon rise, and in retrospect, even the experience of Cambodia I would regret missing. Mr Pin Stripe's snoring I could do without.

Mr Pin Stripe wasn't a bad travel companion. He slept the awkward sleep of the seasoned traveller and talked easy, occasionally irreverent conversation about The Corporation. Both I could cope with. I preferred to keep personal details to myself and was relieved to find he shared this approach. His irreverence amused me, however, he was fond of viciously lampooning those he saw as ineffectual and outdated within The Corporation's military style hierarchy. Those he described as coming from the gin and tonic at the embassy school of international business. Singled out for particular venom was his predecessor the blazer and flannels form of "Tuesday".

Tuesday held himself in very high esteem and was fond of telling anyone at length the tales of his triumphant career. He enjoyed informing me of my lack of prospects within The Corporation and he, a man with excellent prospects, knew about such things. I, in contrast, came from the wrong side of town had been to all the wrong schools and to make it worse: I wore the wrong shoes.

How he came to such an opinion was beyond me. I was surprised he remembered my name we spoke so little. He rarely emerged from his office and when he did preferred to speak Spanish rather than his native English, which made it difficult for me to communicate with him. Most weeks it would be Thursday before Tuesday managed to even say good morning.

Mr Pin Stripe was therefore an improvement, if one who snored like a dying warthog. His grunts and gargles ensured that I remained awake throughout the entire twelve hour flight to Singapore. We had left Heathrow at twelve noon in a blizzard. It was at that time eight pm and thirty degrees Celsius in Singapore. Twelve hours on we arrived at Singapore, my mind thinking it was midnight, only to find it was eight in the morning and the onward flight to Phnom Penh was another five hours away.

Changi Airport was astonishing. It was like walking onto the set of Kubrick's Space Odyssey. The scene early in the film set on the space station orbiting the earth. Vast and clinical, virtually empty with a handful of people wandering slowly through the immaculate sterility as gentle muzak lingered in air.

With jet-lag setting in for the morning I walked through the terminal red eyed and ragged, but enjoying the surreality. If I had bumped into Leonard Rossiter returned from the grave and dressed in the late sixties fashion evident in the film, complete with bad toupee, I would not have been surprised. Spinning though my mind was though, it failed to oblige me with a timely hallucination.

The illusion of being in a classic science fiction movie was maintained as we transferred to another terminal via an efficient and driverless monorail car. The second terminal was again reminiscent of Space Odyssey. I began to suspect that the Singapore government was so impressed with Kubrick's set designer that they hired him to build their airport.

My body ached as I struggled to adjust to an eight hour shift in time zone and meteorological shift from dark skies, sub zero temperatures and a blizzard to brilliant sunshine and a morning temperature of thirty degrees. The air conditioned atmosphere cushioned me from the temperature shift, but exacerbated the disorientation and left my eyes crisp in their sockets as I attempted to sleep on a couch in the Silk Air business lounge and failed.

I splashed cold water on my face and looked into my blood shot eyes in the mirror of the Silk Air business lounge bathroom. My eyes were sore from remaining open for twenty four continuous hours. I tried blinking but they felt loaded with grit. I combed my hair and sprayed my armpits with deodorant — not one of The Corporation's world famous brands, but no one was to know — pulled on a fresh T shirt from my bag and rejoined Mr Pin Stripe in the lounge. He handed me a fresh cup of coffee.

"Is this the woman you worked for in Purchasing?" He passed me a folded A4 brochure card and pointed at a picture of a group of hotel employees standing beneath a sign that read "Welcome to Interfold".

"The Dragon Lady?" I said. "It certainly looks like her. I heard she was running a hotel somewhere these days. Is that the hotel where the conference is being held in Phnom Penh?"

"Certainly is," he said. "Not one I have heard of myself."

"No," I agreed. "Nor me."

Corporate Culture will be published by Burning Eye in 2016

ALSO AVAILABLE BY CLIVE BIRNIE

TERMINAL INSEMINATION ART

(SILKWORMS INK 2012)

CUTTING UP THE ECONOMIST

(BURNINGE EYE 2014)